SISTER SISTER

S. E. GREEN

CHAPTER 1

January, Present Day

With only a sheet covering her, Kinsley Day lay on the rumpled bed, her back to her sister, Lilly, staring at the clock as it flipped to 3:31 in the morning. Beside the clock rested her black-framed reading glasses and a half empty bottle of water. Next to that was Lilly Day's Pulitzer Prize winning novel, *Sister Sister*. They would know for sure tomorrow, but it was expected to hit number one on the *New York Times* Best Sellers list for the two hundredth week in a row.

Aside from Lilly, who softly moaned as she masturbated, the room remained quiet.

Lilly had always been unapologetically sexual.

Though a king size mattress separated the sisters, Kinsley felt Lilly's body quiver as she climaxed. A second or two later, Lilly powered off the vibrator.

Another second or two passed. Lilly sighed, then got up and went to the bathroom.

Kinsley reached for the water bottle. She drank.

Draped on the lounge chair that took up a corner of their room was the pantsuit Kinsley wore to tonight's special viewing of *Sister Sister*. The movie came out last month, but they were in New York for the Oscar nominations announcement. Early critical buzz anticipated it not only to be a shoo-in for Best Picture but to possibly sweep the awards.

The toilet flushed. Kinsley's sister emerged. With rosy cheeks and mussed red hair, Lilly, the "literary phenomenon" as one reviewer called her, stood in boxer shorts and a baggie tee. She might be forty-eight but she easily passed for early thirties. Kinsley shared her hair color and blue eyes, but she looked every bit of her forty-six years.

She attributed that to Lilly.

"I didn't know you were awake," Lilly said.

"Yes."

"Did you hear me—?"

"Yes."

"Ugh, sorry. I'm not used to sharing a room."

The publisher reserved a two-bedroom suite. But Lilly brought her daughters at the last minute, which meant the girls slept in what should have been Kinsley's room.

Sitting up in bed, Kinsley turned on the bedside lamp. Neither one would be sleeping tonight.

Anxious exhaustion drove Lilly's moves as she turned off the bathroom light and walked from their room into the adjoining living room and kitchenette.

Kinsley followed.

From a bountiful gift basket sitting on the kitchen's granite counter, Lilly selected a mini-Pringles can and tore off the seal beneath the cap. She munched the first chip. In the relative silence, the sound filled the room. Her slippered tread whispered as she nervously paced around the living room furniture.

"Do you think Julian's right?" Lilly asked.

Julian, being her agent. "About the Oscars?" Kinsley asked.

Lilly nodded. She munched a second chip, then opened the heavy curtains to reveal Central Park dusted in fresh snow.

"Yes."

"Really?" She ate her third chip.

"Yes."

Lilly moved away from the magnificent view. Eating yet another chip, she walked back into their room. She was climbing the walls. Kinsley was about to suggest she put on workout clothes and go to the hotel gym when Lilly said, "Tell me again what *The New York Times Book Review* said."

From memory, Kinsley recited, "'What makes Lilly Day such a brilliant writer is that she embraces life with an unequivocal passion. Not only does she write with extraordinary depth, but she has also affected generations of writers to come.'"

"That's a lot to live up to," Lilly mumbled.

Kinsley didn't feel that way at all. She considered those words motivation. A challenge to always do better.

"What if it doesn't?" Lilly asked, eating yet another chip.

"Get the nomination?"

Lilly nodded.

"Then it doesn't." Kinsley crawled back onto her side of the bed. "There are only so many things we have control of. This isn't one of them."

"Why are you always so logical?"

Kinsley patted the bed. Lilly came and sat. "Tell you what, if it doesn't happen we'll disappear on some cool adventure. You've always wanted to dive with sharks. Let's do that."

"Really?" Lilly's eyes narrowed. "You, Kinsley Day, are going to dive with sharks?"

"I, Kinsley Day, am going to stay on the boat while *you* dive with sharks."

Lilly laughed, as Kinsley knew she would.

Lilly placed the Pringles can on her bedside table. Kinsley scooted back on the mattress, making space for her older sister. When Lilly nestled against her, Kinsley rubbed her shoulders. Lilly sighed.

"Close your eyes," Kinsley whispered.

Lilly did.

"Deep breaths in and out."

For several moments Lilly breathed while Kinsley's palm stroked her sister's slender back.

Lilly said, "Thank you for taking such good care of me."

"You're welcome."

Taking care of Lilly was what Kinsley did.

―――――

The next morning, the family gathered in the suite's main area to eat breakfast. Over near the vast window Kinsley's fourteen-year-old niece, Tessa, ate a bowl of yogurt and muesli as she took in the panoramic view of Central Park.

Kinsley's twelve-year-old niece, Enid, was curled on the couch reading a book. She'd barely touched her bagel smeared with cranberry chutney.

With dark brown hair and eyes, both girls favored their deceased father.

As usual, Lilly ignored them. Instead, she paced, incessantly checking her phone.

Kinsley sat in a chair, her sock-covered feet propped on an ottoman, drinking coffee and not watching the TV currently running national news. Her phone beeped. Lilly spun to look. Kinsley glanced at the screen.

"Just our security system," Kinsley told her.

Lilly sighed. She paced.

Kinsley brought up the app, seeing multiple views of their sprawling North Florida estate. In contrast to there in New

York, the sun blazed bright, illuminating the twenty thousand square foot property with its outbuildings, lap pool and cabana, a library housing all the various editions and translations of Lilly's work, and an ocean view. *It's a residence appropriate for the world's bestselling novelist.* That's what Lilly's husband, Asher, said when they built it.

Kinsley did think it was pretty, but contracting an over-the-top home was not how she would spend her money. Up until Asher's death five years ago, Kinsley lived in a modest condo. Now she lived with her sister and nieces.

The housekeeper waved into the camera. She mouthed, *Sorry*. Kinsley sent her a quick text to let her know all was good.

"Why hasn't Julian called?" Lilly asked.

"I don't know," Kinsley calmly responded. "Maybe he hasn't heard anything yet."

Lilly checked her phone again. "Nothing is showing up in the news feeds either. What time are they announcing the nominations?"

"I don't know."

She growled. "This is torture!"

"God, Mom." Over near the window, Tessa shoveled a too large heaping of yogurt-covered muesli in her mouth. "Chill the f out."

Enid glanced up from her book. "It's going to be oka—"

A knock sounded at their door.

Lilly gasped. She checked her phone. Laughing, she ran across the suite and flung open the door. Julian stood there dressed in jeans, a beanie, and a thick wool jacket.

"I just saw your text!" Lilly yanked him inside. "I didn't know you were coming over. I've been waiting on your call."

Grinning, Julian brushed his gaze around the family before coming back to Lilly. "First, you made the list. You'll be number one again."

"Yeah, yeah, yeah." Lilly waved that off.

"Second, and most importantly…" Julian's lips pressed together. Kinsley grew still. "Now this is from a secret, high-up source, but we were right! *Sister Sister* has swept the Oscar nominations. They're announcing in sixteen minutes. I wanted you to hear it from me first."

Lilly threw her arms around Julian. They laughed and danced. Pulling away, Lilly looked at Kinsley, her face in delighted shock.

Tessa screamed. She ran to her mom. The two of them laughed and bounced around. Then Julian joined in. The three giddily danced in a circle in the tiny entry space.

One of them shrieked.

In a daze, Enid watched from the couch.

They were all used to the book tours with endless lines of fans awaiting Lilly's presence and signature, to sold out speaking engagements, and even to premieres. But the Oscars? Another whole beast.

Finally, Lilly released them and whirled around. She catapulted herself across the room. She yanked Enid from the couch and Kinsley from the chair. Enid laughed. Lilly pulled them both into a hard embrace.

Julian said, "I highly recommend you don't answer your phone today. We don't want you to get exhausted. Have Kinsley monitor your calls."

As if on cue, Lilly's phone rang.

Into Kinsley's ear, Lilly uttered, "It was all worth it."

To that, Kinsley made no response.

CHAPTER 2

*S*eptember, *Thirty Years Ago*

I sit in the back left corner of an overcrowded tenth-grade English class. I hear we no longer have a teacher. I don't blame her for leaving. I would've walked off the job as well after being cussed out by not one, but three foul-mouthed high school girls too old to still be in this class.

Saying I attend the worst high school in Jacksonville, Florida, puts it lightly. But I have no choice. My and Lilly's latest group home is zoned this school. At nearly eighteen, Lilly graduates this year, which means she'll age out of the system. Our case worker's doing everything she can to make sure Lilly gets guardianship of me. Then we can move into our own apartment.

What we'll do then, I don't know. Lilly wants to go to college and study writing. Her grades aren't great though. I'm not sure how she's going to pull that off.

Up front, a girl blares loud rap music.

A giant ball of paper flies through the air.

A clump of students stand on their desks, gyrating.

The girl seated in front of me draws on her bare arm with a Sharpie.

Oddly enough, this class has only two boys. They, too, sit in the back, each huddled under their hoodie as they take a nap.

In a normal school, someone would come to check on us. But it's been ten minutes and nothing.

It's not like me to leave, but I'll give it five more and then exit quietly. I'd much rather be in the pitiful excuse of a room called our library than here.

A young, tall and broad, stunningly beautiful man walks in. With sun kissed skin, light brown hair, and eyes so green they seem to glow, he walks to the teacher's desk. He stands, calmly taking in the disorderly scene.

One by one the girls gradually realize there's a teacher. If it had been anyone other than this god of a man, my classmates wouldn't care. But the music turns off. The gyrating girls slowly lower themselves into their chairs. Miss Sharpie Pen pauses. A few get nudged. Hell, the worst of the girls even clasps her hands and sits up straight. Cleavage pushes out. Legs seductively cross. A hush falls over the raucous class.

Placing his beat up brown satchel on the metal desk, the man smiles widely.

I blink.

Even his teeth are vividly white and perfectly placed.

"My name's Niko Young. I'm sorry I'm late. Honestly, I got lost."

A round of giggles floats through the air.

"In case you're wondering, I am not your sub. I will be your tenth-grade English teacher."

His hypnotic voice captivates me.

"Now who can tell me what book we're reading."

Silence.

My classmates look around.

His gaze rolls across the room.

Slowly, my hand goes up. My voice comes much more confident than usual. "We're currently reading *The Grapes of Wrath*."

My classmates turn. All attention falls on me. But I don't look at any of them. I stare directly at Niko Young.

I swallow.

"Ah. Who is the author?"

"J—" I clear my throat. "John Steinbeck."

In my peripheral, I see a girl size me up. Though I've always attended rough schools, I've never developed a tough demeanor. I do well hovering in the shadows. It's how I've managed to not get beat up. In contrast, Lilly's out there. She's not been in a lot of fights but enough to earn her a level of respect. If anyone respects me, it's only because of her.

I don't speak out in class. I don't make eye contact with anyone. I fly under the radar. But at this moment, with Niko Young focused on me, I sit up straighter. I ignore the glaring girl. I maintain eye contact, feeling a boldness and power I've never experienced before.

"I guess you're getting the first extra credit point." His attention moves off of me. "We'll be studying some great writing this year but doing a bit of it ourselves. The only thing I require is that you write with rawness. Don't give me something you think I want to read. Give me something you *don't* think I want to read. Write as if your very soul depends on it."

He turns away, opening his satchel and bringing out *The Grapes of Wrath*. He turns back and with a fierce gaze nods to me. "Your name?"

"Kinsley Day."

"Well, Kinsley Day, read aloud page one."

The class continues in perfect order as he nods to random

students asking their names and instructing them to read page two, page five, page seven…

When the bell rings, students file out, most stopping to "innocently" flirt.

Quietly, I leave out the back.

I've had crap teachers in equally crap schools. But something tells me I was destined to meet Mr. Young.

CHAPTER 3

J anuary, Present Day

That night after the big Oscar announcements, they attended a party in honor of Lilly Day put on by her publisher. Industry professionals gathered in the trendy, rented-out restaurant artfully decorated with mosaic tiles and black and white framed photos of the city. It was an intimate group made up of the publishing team and a few local authors who wrote for the same house. The celebratory atmosphere came relaxed with most dressed in jeans and sports coats, skirts and leggings.

Near the buffet table, Julian placed a select amount of appetizers on his plate. At the bar the publisher smothered Lilly, lavishing his star writer with attention.

Holding a glass of merlot, Kinsley stood along the far wall with her nieces. Tessa scrolled through her phone. Enid yawned. They were as bored as Kinsley. She hated these things. She'd rather be back at the hotel reading, watching Netflix, or just about anything else.

Julian approached. He surveyed the three of them as he popped an olive into his mouth. "You three look like a lively bunch. How are my Florida girls holding up in this freezing weather?"

"We're fine," Kinsley said.

"We'll be out in LA for the Oscars," Julian said. He glanced at the front bank of windows revealing no fresh snow but lots of dark sludge. "It'll probably *still* be snowing here." He ate another olive.

Kinsley liked Julian enough, but let's face it, Lilly Day's success made his career.

Lilly stepped up beside Julian and stage-whispered, "I just found out I'm going to be on the cover of *Time*."

"Yes," Julian preened, "I secured that for you. I was waiting to tell you." He gave a mock scowl toward the publisher, still at the bar and now speaking with a local author. "Looks like someone opened his big mouth."

Lilly laughed.

Tessa kept scrolling her phone. "How much longer do we have to stay?" she griped without taking her eyes off the device.

Lilly sent Kinsley a "you handle her" look.

"Not much," Kinsley said.

"I don't mind staying," Enid softly spoke.

"That's because you're my favorite," Lilly teased, gently pinching her chin.

Enid blushed.

"Blah, blah, blah." Tessa kept scrolling.

Julian detailed the party attendees. Idly, Lilly listened as she took the glass of wine from Kinsley's fingers and sipped. A little bit dribbled on her white cardigan.

"*No.*" She dabbed at it with a napkin. "This is cashmere."

Tessa put her phone away. "I think your bigger problem is that it's white."

"Let me get some soda water." Julian snapped his fingers at a waiter.

Lilly kept dabbing, making it worse.

Kinsley took the glass from her fingers and set it aside. "Soda water won't help. Come with me."

"Where are we going?"

"To the bathroom to give you my outfit."

———

"Thank God we're about the same size." Lilly tugged Kinsley's gray sweater dress into place. Next came her black leggings followed by black ankle boots.

In the mirror, Lilly surveyed herself. "It's not my style but it'll have to do." She smoothed a few flyaway hairs.

Kinsley stood behind her in the wine splotched sweater and burgundy pants that fit her too snugly. She didn't know why Lilly always wore such formfitting clothes. Kinsley preferred to breathe.

In the mirror, Lilly studied Kinsley. "Tell me this is our life."

"No denying it."

Someone knocked. "Lilly?" Julian called. "We're ready when you are."

Turning to look at Kinsley, Lilly asked, "How do I look?"

Kinsley stoically imitated *AbFab's* Patsy Stone. "Fabulous, darling."

Lilly laughed. She walked out first. Kinsley followed.

Julian directed Lilly over to the corner where a microphone stood on a tiny stage. A bit over-the-top for such an intimate gathering, but whatever.

Kinsley found Tessa at the buffet table, picking through a charcuterie board as she held a conversation with one of the other authors in attendance. Tessa laughed in this capable and confident way that sounded exactly like Lilly. In contrast,

Enid had already escaped to the shadowed corner where she stood silently, taking the party in.

So intelligent and tortured, little Enid.

Of Kinsley's two nieces, she felt closest to the youngest. She understood Enid.

Kinsley walked to her. "Not much longer and we'll scram. Cool?"

"Cool." Enid sipped her cola.

Leaning against the wall, Kinsley's gaze made a lazy track across the room.

"I, um, gave Mom a short story I wrote." Awkwardly, Enid cleared her throat. "Two weeks ago."

"She's been busy. Want me to remind her?"

"No," Enid quickly replied.

"I read it. I hope you don't mind."

Surprised, Enid turned to Kinsley. "You did?"

"I saw it in her inbox. I peeked. Beautifully written, Enid. A smart piece."

"Really?"

"I wouldn't lie."

Enid's shoulders relaxed. "Well, don't say anything to Mom. I don't have a thick enough skin if she hates it."

"She won't hate it."

"Still, don't say anything. Promise?"

"I promise."

Julian tapped the microphone. Beside him, Lilly stood with *Sister Sister* in its original artfully simple cover with the Pulitzer sticker affixed to the front.

Kinsley gathered her nieces and went to stand nearer to the small stage.

The crowd had grown since they first arrived. Everyone organized themselves, growing quiet and looking toward Lilly. Kinsley put an arm around each niece, giving them both a little squeeze.

Lilly collected her thoughts. "I want to thank you all for

being here tonight and celebrating all the great news surrounding this novel. I'm humbled. I'm happy. I'm honored my publishing team is here and I'm especially grateful my sister, Kinsley, is in attendance along with my proudest achievements—my daughters Tessa and Enid. I only wish their father was here to celebrate with us."

She paused a moment. A fond smile curved her lips.

"My family's been blessed with all my books hitting the list, the majority at number one. We've been delighted to see many adapted for the screen. This one though has always been different. It was one of those novels that sat on the back burner for years, just waiting for the right time." She lifted the book. "And here it is."

Lilly looked at Kinsley. "Dear sister, I know you don't like the fact I'm putting eyes on you but you need to know that I would not be here without you. From foster homes to group homes to sharing our first roach-infested apartment, to switching outfits with me when I'm a klutz, it's always been you and me. We took on the world, and dare I say that we're winning."

The crowd chuckled.

"I'd be nothing without your support. I love you."

Everyone let out a collective *aw*.

Kinsley forced her lips into what she hoped appeared like a pleasant smile. Lilly thought saying words like "family" and "we" made her look self-effacing. Kinsley thought it made her look like a narcissistic twat.

Julian raised a glass. "To Lilly Day!"

CHAPTER 4

September, Thirty Years Ago

My sister didn't have Niko Young but she saw him walking the halls.

"I heard you have a new teacher," she said, flopping across my bed. "Did you know he's only twenty-two? He's practically *my* age. Do you think he's married?"

I shrugged. "He's not wearing a ring."

"Girlfriend?"

Another shrug. "You have a boyfriend, though."

"Whatever." Lilly leaned in. "Hot for teacher is my new spank bank." She laughed.

I forced a smile, as I always did at her uncouth comments and humor.

"Well anyway, there's a short story contest worth cash plus a partial scholarship to the University of North Florida. Will you read what I wrote?" she asked.

"Of course."

She swung off my bed. "I already printed it for you."

That was on Monday of last week and she has appeared at my fifth-period English class every day since with a smug glow about her. Like she already owns this man's heart and soul.

Hello, Mr. Young. I'm Kinsley's big sister. If you have any problems with her, just let me know.

Hi, Mr. Young, you having a good day?

Mr. Young, I like that tie!

Howdy, Mr. Young. Just here to walk my baby sister to her next class.

Mr. Young, did I see you at Winn Dixie?

Hey, if you're looking for a teacher's aide, I come highly recommended.

That last comment comes today, Friday, as she boldly walks into my classroom.

"Thank you, Lilly, but I'm fine." Mr. Young looks at me. "Kinsley, if you don't mind I'd like a minute." He cuts back over to my sister. "Lilly, you can wait in the hall."

His request startles her, but she expertly plasters a grin and struts out. More than one girl shoots me an envious glare. When the class empties he puts my yellow journal on top of his desk. Journaling's new to me. He gave each classmate one—in various colors—asking us to write a minimum of once per week. I've written every single day. He collects them on Friday and gives them back on Monday. The fact he's giving mine back now throws me off.

Out in the hall, a girl shrieks with laughter. Inside this room, I barely breathe as I wait for him to speak. Did I do something wrong? Why does he want to see me?

"I read this during today's test. I couldn't wait. I knew it would be good."

His words should alleviate my growing anxiety, but they don't.

He sits down, leaving me standing with a desk between

us. Quietly, he studies me through those spellbinding green eyes. One day I'm going to write about those eyes.

He says, "You and your sister are two very different young women."

"Yes."

"I'm sorry you lost your parents." He taps the journal. "That was a tremendously moving passage."

I don't respond. We were in the car the night they died. I was only six but I'll never forget the lights flashing, the spinning car, the screaming, the horn blaring, the emergency team prying me and Lilly from the back, the social worker telling us our parents had died.

"What do you want to do when you grow up?" Niko asks.

Huh. I never really thought of that. My world tends to orbit Lilly's desires, not mine. "My sister wants to be a famous novelist."

"Writing runs in the family, huh?"

"Yeah, I guess."

"Your sister wants to be a famous novelist. But what do *you* want to do?"

"Survive."

His arms fold. He sits back. He watches me intently. "That's an interesting response."

My attention flits up to the round clock hanging on the wall. My next class is only a few rooms down. Still, I don't want to be late. It's open seating and I'll get stuck in the front if I am.

"Kinsley."

"Yes?"

"There's an intelligence and depth to your writing far beyond your years. Yet there's also a detachment which is an interesting twist."

I'm not sure how he expects me to respond. So, I force a smile just like I do with Lilly when she complains that I don't "feel" anything, that I'm too "stoic," that I'm one of those "implosive" people who will one day shoot up the world.

"I'm going to be late for my next class."

The intensity of his stare gentles to kindness. Or more like an endearment. I glance over to where my sister stares at me through the small glass window.

"Can I go?" I ask.

There's a pause, then, "Yes, of course." He slides the yellow journal toward me. "You can take that now."

I grab it and just as quickly leave the room.

Out in the hall, Lilly's in my face. "What did he want?"

"Nothing." I walk toward my next class. "He asked me what I wanted to do when I grow up."

"That's all?"

"Yes."

"Oh... well, I'll see you later."

In my next class period I, unfortunately, am left sitting in front. I place the journal on top of my desk. While the teacher calls roll, I open the journal's front cover, intending to reread the passage that Mr. Young spoke of. Instead, I find a hand-written message across the first page. I trail my finger over the words.

Promise me you'll keep writing.

CHAPTER 5

arch, *Present Day*

The line to get signatures stretched out the indie book store and down several Los Angeles blocks. Readers camped out all night waiting for a personalized copy with not only Lilly's name but the lead actresses in the *Sister Sister* adaptation.

A long table separated the stars from the crowd. Books were stacked on the table, waiting to be personalized by the three of them. Two assistants worked at taking names, writing them on yellow sticky notes and affixing them to the front cover. Three other assistants held books open for autographs, providing fresh Sharpies every ten minutes or so. Another assistant bustled around, getting Lilly and the two movie stars water and whatever else.

A well-oiled machine.

Beneath Lilly's chair, candy wrappers littered the floor where she snuck peppermints every so often.

Kinsley stood ensconced between a magazine rack and Julian. She didn't usually come to Lilly's signings, at least not anymore. But Lily had been unusually nervous this morning and begged Kinsley to join her.

"Please," Lilly said. "If only for a little while."

So, Kinsley left Tessa and Enid at the hotel and here she stood.

Lilly laughed at something a reader just commented on. She posed for a picture.

"She's really on today," Julian commented.

"Yes, she is." Which made Kinsley wonder why she even needed her.

Smiling, a twenty-something boyish man stepped up, staring at Lilly. Tall and lean with dark hair and rimless glasses, he had that fresh glow of adoration for this author he idolized. Given he wore a sizable backpack, Kinsley assumed he camped out overnight just for these few seconds of being in Lilly's presence.

He was just her type.

After getting the two actresses' signatures, he stood in front of Lilly. His eyes lit up. "Ms. Day, I am delighted to meet you."

An assistant passed her a book, open and ready. Lilly read the name on the sticky note and quickly personalized the interior page. She glanced up and there it happened—the flare of quiet interest.

Quickly she glanced at the sticky note. "And I'm delighted to meet you, *Steven*."

"All of your books are great, but this one is an astounding achievement."

"Thank you, Steven. Are you a writer?"

A fresh blush brightened his cheeks. "I am."

She floated a hand through the air. "Know that it's not about all of this. It's about writing from the heart. You do that and you stay true to yourself."

"Absolutely."

She slid the book across the table, making sure their

fingers brushed. An assistant expertly moved Steven along. Kinsley observed all of this with practiced readiness when Lilly cut her "the look."

Quietly, Kinsley excused herself from Julian. She followed Steven through the packed bookstore. He already paid for the book and he held it to his chest as he walked out into the sunshine. He cut left, trailing along the line of people waiting their turn. At the crosswalk, he paused, opening the book and tracing her signature. The crosswalk light blinked green.

When he made it to the other side and out of earshot of the fans, Kinsley approached him. "Excuse me?"

He whirled around, surprised. "Yes?"

"I'm Kinsley Day, Lilly's sister." She held out a hand. "It's nice to meet you."

"Oh my gosh." Excitedly, he shook her hand. He showed her the book. "She just signed this!"

"I know." Kinsley gave a friendly smile.

"I'm sure she hears this all the time but the book is way better than the movie."

"I don't know about that," Kinsley teased. "It's rumored the movie will dominate the Oscars next week."

"Oh, it will. I have no doubt."

Kinsley kept her friendliness in check. "By any chance are you free tonight?"

The question took him off guard. "Um…yes."

"You made quite the impression on Lilly. She'd like to know if you're available for a drink later."

His brown eyes widened. He fumbled for words. "A-are you serious?"

"I am serious."

"Yes! Oh my God, yes. Where? When?"

She gave him the name of their hotel, a time, and told him to meet Lilly in the lounge. Of course, nine times out of ten the drink led to Lilly's bed.

Steven stood frozen in delighted shock. Leaving him there,

Kinsley turned away. Her smile slid as she backtracked through the crosswalk and trailed the line inching forward.

Once inside the bookstore, she resumed her place next to Julian.

Lilly glanced over. Kinsley nodded. And with a vague stare, she watched the rest of her afternoon tick by.

———

It was much later than expected when they walked into the grand and luxurious hotel lobby. Smiling, a doorman nodded his head as they passed. Looking as rumpled and tired as Kinsley felt, Lilly eyed a clump of people across the lobby looking back. Their eyes shined in awe.

Quietly, she sighed. "The hotel is supposed to be my safe space."

Julian squeezed her arm. "I'll get rid of them and then talk to the manager."

"No, I'm good."

Lilly handed Kinsley her purse as she walked toward the adoring readers ready to lavish her with more attention. Books came out. Pens shoved forward. Phones snapped pictures. It seemed to reinvigorate her as she eagerly began signing yet more autographs.

Kinsley stood back, holding Lilly's purse as well as her own. Her feet hurt. Her stomach needed food. But her expression settled into one of supportive pride—as any good entourage member would look. She waited for the initial flush of her sister's arrival to die down so they could get the girls, eat dinner, and call it a day.

She spotted her nieces over in the lobby's sitting area, both scowling at their mother. Kinsley crossed to them, gladly slumping into a loveseat. She placed both purses on the cushion beside her. She looked at Tessa first, then Enid, both in wide armed chairs.

"Want to know a secret?" Kinsley asked.

They were already smiling.

"I would shave my head for a banana split." Kinsley's stomach growled.

"Can't we go to dinner without her?" Tessa whined. "We've been waiting *forever*."

"Give it ten minutes. Then we'll go without her."

Tessa eyed both purses. "Got any gum?"

Kinsley fished some out, giving both girls a piece and taking one for herself.

Enid pondered her mom as she unwrapped the gum. "Do you think she likes being swamped like that?"

"I think she knows it's part of the job."

"What if it were you?" Enid asked.

"Let's just say it's a good thing that it's not me. I would not do well being constantly smothered. I would be the worst famous person ever."

"Not me," Tessa bragged. "I'd handle it like a boss."

True. She would.

The crowd around Lilly grew larger. Tessa noticed. "Let's just go without her. Ten minutes from now it's only going to get worse."

As if on cue, Lilly's jovial voice carried across the lobby. "My family is over there, waiting patiently for me to eat dinner. As much as I adore you all, my stomach is rudely reminding me that I need nourishment. AKA, a giant cheeseburger."

Delighted laughter filled the air at the warm and witty Lilly Day.

Julian took that as his cue to sweep into the magic circle and usher Lilly out. Some followed as he led her across the lobby toward her family. He saw her to them before redirecting to handle the stragglers.

An elegant and put-together woman dressed in a business suit approached. "Ms. Day, I'm Blake Fitzroy, the hotel manager. It is an honor to meet you. I so admire your work." She extended a hand and they shook. "I apologize for that. It won't happen again. We'd like to comp your dinner tonight here at our restaurant. That is if you don't already have plans."

Standing, Kinsley shook hands with the manager as well. "That would be great, thank you. This is the one night that Lilly doesn't have plans, so that works perfectly."

"I'll let them know to keep a table open for you." With a polite nod, the manager backed away.

"Can we go now?" Tessa moaned.

"That's fine with me." Kinsley said, noting Lilly ignoring them as she stared into the adjacent lounge. A young bartender stood, shaking a martini, gazing at Lilly as she, more than intrigued, returned his interest.

An exchange not lost on Kinsley.

"Mom?" Enid touched her arm. "Dinner?"

"Hm?" Lilly turned away from the bartender. She put a distracted hand on her daughter's shoulder. "Of course. Yes, of course. Food. Now."

"You all go ahead." Kinsley waved them on. "I'll catch up."

When the three of them loaded onto the elevator, Kinsley made her way over to the bartender where she proceeded to arrange tomorrow's hookup for her sister.

———

After dinner, they walked into their lavishly appointed suite. Tessa and Enid cut off to their shared room. Gift baskets and flowers lined the coffee table, the window sills, the kitchen counter, and every other available space.

"Do you mind searching all these for some chocolate?" Lilly asked.

Kinsley surveyed the gift baskets as Lilly crossed the suite and entered her bedroom. It was a grand room dominated by a giant bed and complete with a sitting area, a large desk, an entertainment center, and several dressers.

Kinsley found Lilly in the walk-in closet.

"What time am I meeting tonight's guy?" Lilly asked.

"His name is Steven. You're meeting him at ten in the lounge downstairs. That's one hour from now." Kinsley handed her a chocolate-covered caramel. As Lilly undressed and simultaneously ate the caramel, Kinsley took out her wallet. She showed her sister a card key. "I got you a room on the fifth floor: 503. I'll put the key in your wallet."

Lilly slid into a silk robe. She moved past Kinsley and over to a dresser where she selected lingerie. "What about the bartender?"

"Not really your type."

"I know." Lilly crinkled her nose. "I don't typically go for the handsome blond. I'm all about the dark haired nerd. Bonus if he has glasses. But the bartender does scream sex. So…"

Whatever.

"His name is Christian and you two are on for tomorrow." Kinsley followed her sister across the expansive room and into the bathroom. With a shower, a tub, toilet, bidet, two sinks, warming racks, and a closet, it was bigger than their first apartment. "I'm sure you'll see Christian at the bar tonight."

"Perfect, if things don't work out with Steven, I'll see if Christian wants to be bumped up." She stripped and stepped into the shower. "What about you?"

"What do you mean?" Kinsley selected shower gel from the products lined up on the counter and gave it to Lilly.

"What do you mean what do I mean? You going to get laid?"

"You know how much I hate when you ask me that."

"*Sorry*. Geez."

"Listen, I'm tired. Do you need anything else?"

"Are you okay? You seem off to—oh my God!" Lilly slid open the glass shower door. She showed Kinsley her teeth. "How long has that green glob been there!"

"I don't know."

Lilly grabbed the shower mirror and grinned into it. "Ugh! It's right there." She picked at it with her nail. "It's not coming out."

"I'll find you some floss." Kinsley searched the bathroom drawers. "I wouldn't worry about it. Everyone glowed in your presence. No one noticed a tiny fleck of green."

The water went off. Lilly took a few seconds to dry off. Wrapped in a towel, she stepped out. "I think it's in my makeup bag."

"Why do you put floss in your makeup bag?"

"Because I do. Why do you care where I put my floss?"

"It's a stupid place to put floss. Makeup goes in a makeup bag. Floss goes in with your dental bag. That's why I bought you separate bags for everything."

"Ugh, you're so annoying." Lilly scooted past her and back into the bedroom

Kinsley opened Lilly's makeup bag. Sure enough, finding floss. She began to zip the bag when something caught her eye.

In the interior pouch protected by clear plastic nestled a beaded necklace that Kinsley made Lilly back when their parents were still alive. How did Kinsley not know that Lilly kept this?

Carefully, Kinsley took it out. She noted the silver tag that their father attached before she gave it to Lilly. Faded now from decades gone by, the etched lettering barely read two words:

Forever Sisters

CHAPTER 6

ovember, *Thirty Years Ago*

I stand on the porch of a modest stucco home belonging to Dr. Wilkes. A professor at the University of North Florida, he's on the committee that will pick the winner of the writing competition Lilly entered.

"Guess what?" My sister's face lights up with excited mischievousness. "I've got a plan to push my short story through."

I didn't like her look or her tone, but here I am.

The door flies open. Lilly stands there, frazzled, holding a crying baby. She shoves the kid into my arms. "My God, I am never having children."

Leaving me to find my way, she charges back inside.

I look at the kid, her tiny face streaked with tears. I pat her back. "There, there." I step inside. "What's your name?"

She hiccups. A few more tears bubble up and over.

It's a messy house with toys, clothes, and various other things strewn about. As I walk through the living room, the baby's crying gradually subsides. I find my sister in a kitchen in dire need of cleaning. "What's her name?" I ask.

"Beats me."

"You agreed to babysit a kid and you don't know her name?"

"Yes." Impatiently, she opens the refrigerator, grabs an open bottle of white wine, and pours herself a glass.

I spy a bottle of milk on the top shelf, retrieve it, and warm it in the microwave. While I wait, I check the baby's diaper. Thankfully, it's clean. I also note an emergency list taped to the refrigerator with the child's name at the top.

The microwave dings. I double-check the milk isn't too hot. Then I give it to the baby. "There you go, Grace."

Eagerly, she sucks.

My sister watches. "Who would've thought you'd be the baby whisperer."

Gently, I rock her.

"Okay, phase one's set. I answered their ad. I am their new babysitter. He, of course, has no idea I'm one of the competition writers. That'll come later. Also—" she grins— "They were in a horrible fight when I got here about how messy this house is. All the better." She points to a family photo hanging on the wall. "Check out how homely Mrs. Wilkes is. He'll welcome my advances, believe me."

It's always an elaborate plan with Lilly.

She puts her glass down. "Follow me."

Holding Grace, I trail behind my sister through the kitchen, across the living room, and down a narrow hall. We step into the Wilkeses' unkempt bedroom. I don't like intruding on their personal space. Lilly walks inside the closet, taking a second to peer at the couple's clothes.

She wanders around the room, opening and closing dresser drawers and rifling through both nightstands. In the bathroom, she does the same.

I watch her, knowing one hundred percent this is wrong,

and doing nothing about it. Still, I ask, "What are you looking for?"

"Toys. Vibrators. Lube. Dildos. Lingerie." She holds up roomie white panties, cringing. "Oh yeah, Professor Wilkes will be all into my kink." She puts everything back. At my disapproving expression, she rolls her eyes. "What, it's not like I'm asking you to service the professor. I'm taking one for the team. It's a scholarship, Kinsley, plus enough money to get an apartment. It's our ticket to better things. Believe me, he's not the first professor to be seduced by a co-ed."

"You don't need all of this. That story's good. It'll win without you 'taking one for the team.'"

My sister sighs.

Her reckless expression instantly softens. She comes to me, lightly placing her hand on the baby's head. She caresses the infant's soft hair. "You're right, the submission's good. It's great even. Think of this as insurance. We've been dealt a shit life. I'll do whatever it takes to get us a leg up." She presses a kiss on my cheek. "Your only job's to back me up. Okay?"

Grace finishes the bottle. I hand it to my sister, pick up a man's undershirt off the bed, and lay it and Grace over my shoulder. I pat her back. She drools. My sister winces.

"Okay?" she repeats.

"Fine."

CHAPTER 7

arch, *Present Day*

The sun rose as Kinsley emerged from her room. She crossed the quiet suite, her footsteps soft, coming to stand at the floor to ceiling windows. She took several seconds to gaze out at the warm light drifting over Beverly Hills.

In the kitchenette, she selected two white mugs and poured coffee from the timed pot. She added regular cream to both.

Back across the suite she quietly entered Lilly's room. Kinsley didn't know when her sister got in last night, but she hoped not too late. Lilly had a Zoom interview in one hour with a reporter on the east coast.

A thick white comforter smothered Lilly's body. Kinsley placed one of the mugs on the bedside table and moved to swivel open the vertical blinds.

"Time to get up. You've got an interview in one hour."

Lilly moaned and stirred. With a yawn, she sat up. As she

did, the comforter rustled, revealing a second person buried in the pile of high thread count linens.

Christian, the bartender.

He rolled over, snagging Lilly around the waist and pulling her underneath him. She woke up then with a startled yelp.

"Out!" She shoved his shoulders. "You've got to leave."

Christian laughed.

"I'm not kidding." Lilly squirmed.

Loudly, Kinsley cleared her throat.

Christian froze.

Slowly, he looked over at Kinsley, just now realizing she was in the room.

Lilly shoved at his shoulders again. "Now, go."

On the floor at the foot of the bed laid his clothes. Kinsley picked them up and handed them to Christian. Then she stepped from the room.

Back in the kitchenette, Kinsley sipped her coffee and stared at the girls' door. Of the two sisters, Enid rose early. She would be affected the most by seeing a man leave their suite. Kinsley stared, hoping it didn't open.

It did.

But Enid didn't emerge. Tessa did at the exact second Christian stumbled from Lilly's room.

Both Tessa and Christian came up short. Kinsley opened the door that led into the hall, silently telling him to get the hell out. He did, without a word.

Lilly hurried into the main area. "I am so sorry. The key to my other room didn't work. We came back here. I set my alarm—" Her voice cut off when she noticed Tessa standing there uncharacteristically mute.

As usual, Lilly turned to Kinsley for help.

Lilly's sex life was the number one thing to be kept private and separate from the girls. For this exact reason.

"Go get ready for your interview," Kinsley told her sister.

Lilly gladly and quickly did.

Silently, Tessa approached the kitchenette. She slid onto an island stool. Kinsley poured her niece coffee and added one teaspoon of natural sugar.

With Enid, she required gentle prodding in tense situations. Tessa, on the other hand, would speak when ready. Given this, Kinsley took her time making oatmeal.

Quiet seconds rolled by.

It didn't take Tessa long. "Does Mom usually have 'other rooms' when we travel with her?"

Kinsley tried her best to always be truthful with her nieces. If Kinsley told her to ask her mother, Lilly would do what she always did—ignore and redirect things back to Kinsley.

"Your mother has a very healthy sex life. What she does in private is her business. Just like what you do in private is your business."

"Does she miss Dad?"

"Yes, very much. Your parents loved each other deeply."

"Did she have 'other rooms' with Dad?"

"No, never," Kinsley lied.

"Don't you ever get tired?"

"Of what?"

"Being her keeper?"

CHAPTER 8

arch, *Twenty-Nine Years Ago*

The final bell rings. Students crowd the hall, ushering out for the day. At my locker, I pause to read what Mr. Young wrote in my journal.

I love the shape of your stories.

My sister bumps into me from behind. She wraps an arm around my upper body and loudly kisses my cheek. Quickly, I store the journal and close my locker. I turn to see her grinning.

"What?" I ask.

She squeals. "Guess who won the contest? Guess who snagged a scholarship from said contest? Guess who's getting a nice fat check?"

"I knew it." I hug her.

She slings an arm around my neck and leads me through the crowded hall. "We're going to the campus this weekend to walk around. We're also going to look at apartments. Plus on that side of the city, you'll be zoned for an A-plus school. You're officially getting out of this hellhole."

"Oh, wow."

"Yep." With an arm still around me, she leads me down the sidewalk toward our bus.

All around kids shove us, cuss words pound the air, a fight breaks out, loud rap music thumps. We board our bus, sitting beside each other. As Lilly freshens her lip gloss, I glance out the window to see Mr. Young in the teacher's lot unlocking his battered gray car. As if sensing my stare, he glances up, giving a tiny wave.

I wave back.

"Who are you waving at?" Lilly asks, moving on to redoing her mascara.

"Mr. Young."

"What a waste of man. I did everything but strip naked and he could care less. He's probably gay."

That's her reasoning for every handsome guy who isn't interested in her advances.

She puts away her mascara. "Let's get ice cream and celebrate."

"Deal."

The bus pulls away. We ride a short distance to our group home. Along with three other girls, we get off. The bus moves on. The other girls walk toward the old white brick building.

We stroll in the opposite direction toward the convenience store where we always buy our celebratory ice creams.

A woman approaches, fast, from across the cracked pavement. Looking bedraggled, much older than I'm sure she is, and frenzied with anger, she barks Lilly's name with so much force that we freeze.

"Mrs. Wilkes? What are you doing he—"

The woman slaps my sister across the face. "You little bitch."

I step forward, grabbing Mrs. Wilkes's arm. "Hey."

She yanks from my grasp. She jabs a finger into Lilly's face. "Stay away from my husband. Do you hear me?"

"Yes," Lilly quickly answers. "Yes, I hear you."

"If I see you anywhere near him ever again, I will kill you." She shoots a furious gaze my way before spinning and madly charging off. My sister stands stunned, watching Professor Wilkes's wife climb into her car and drive away.

For several seconds Lilly doesn't move. Neither do I.

Lilly's affair with Professor Wilkes has been going on since about a month after I went to his house that night to help her babysit. After that night, she sat for them every two weeks or so. I always helped, making sure to leave before the Wilkeses returned. Professor Wilkes drove Lilly home on those evenings. Their affair mostly occurred in his car.

It had been going on for two months when he said, "I just read a story written by Lilly Day."

Lilly blinked, innocent. "What are you talking about? The contest I entered?"

"I'm on the committee that picks the winner."

"Oh?" Slowly, she straddled him. "You do what you must, but I would never ask for favoritism." She kissed his neck.

"The essay was good, Lilly. No favoritism needed."

She undid his zipper and pulled him out.

That's when I stopped listening to her recant his discovery of who she was.

Now, I move, stepping in front of her. Red mars her cheek where Mrs. Wilkes slapped her. "You okay?" I ask.

Turning away, Lilly takes a few breaths.

Then she's back—every bit as confident and self-assured as always. She tosses her red hair. She loops her arm through mine. She tugs me down the sidewalk in the direction we'd been going before all of this happened.

"I won't lose the scholarship or the money over this. We're

okay. We're good. I did what I had to." Her pace quickens. "You want rocky road or praline?"

"Lilly?"

"Hm."

"Promise me you won't do something like that again."

She stops walking. "I won't make that promise because it's you and me, Kinsley. Against the world. You've got my back; I've got yours. We're a team. One day it'll be your turn to sacrifice and you'll do it without question."

CHAPTER 9

arch, Present Day

After Kinsley talked to Tessa about her mom's overnight guest, Enid woke up. Tessa told her younger sister what happened, leaving Kinsley to answer all of Enid's questions as well as more from Tessa. With little time to shower and dress, Kinsley barely made it to Lilly's Zoom interview.

Kinsley stood off camera watching Lilly regale the reporter with one of her favorite anecdotes. "It was our first apartment. I was writing, in longhand mind you, my first novel. We had no heat, a roach problem, and one can of *SpaghettiOs* to our name. Kinsley comes in all bothered about something that happened at school. She starts taking it out on the roaches. She kills one with a book. Another with a pot. A third with the can of *SpaghettiOs*. She was like a highly trained roach assassin. She just kept wiping the guts on her jeans and killing the next one. The whole time I kept writing. When she finished she made us the *SpaghettiOs* and I calmly said, 'Tomorrow I'll get us some roach motels.'"

The reporter laughed and laughed in this jovial, toothy way. Kinsley hated that barely true story. But everyone seemed to love it, so Lilly continued to tell it.

"Well, Ms. Day, it has been such a privilege spending the past thirty minutes with you. My last question is about your family. Any up and coming writers we should know about?"

Lilly glanced at Kinsley who nodded for her to look back at the camera. With cheeriness, Lilly did saying, "My youngest daughter is quite talented. She's got a unique voice."

"Perhaps one day we'll see her name beside yours in the bookstores. Or the two of you will write a book together."

"Yes, perhaps."

The interview ended.

Lilly closed the laptop screen. "Well, she annoyed me. If I had to look at her tragic buckteeth one more second I was going to offer to buy her Invisalign."

"We need to talk about earlier," Kinsley said.

Standing, Lilly moved away from her and over to a wall-mounted mirror. She inspected her neck. "Next time let's set me up in front of the windows. The lighting in here is terrible. Did you see my neck? I kept shifting to get it out of the shadows. It makes my skin look crepey."

Lilly's bedroom door opened and Enid peeked in. *All clear?* she mouthed.

"Yes." Kinsley waved her on.

Hesitantly, she approached. "I listened to the interview. I hope you don't mind."

Smiling, Lilly looked at her youngest daughter in the mirror. "Of course not. What did you think?"

"Did you..." Enid nibbled her bottom lip. She glanced at Kinsley before going back to her mom. "Did you mean it about me having a unique voice?"

Lilly kept inspecting her neck. "Sure I meant it."

"Good enough to one day be in a bookstore like you?"

"Well, now, I don't want to get your hopes up. Just because a reporter suggested it doesn't make it so. A good majority of people write their whole lives and never see anything published. You've got to have a thick skin and dedication." She turned away from the mirror, looking at Kinsley. "What's next on my schedule?"

Enid took a step closer. "But the first novel you wrote became a hit. That might be me, right?"

"It's better to be rooted in reality. Your Aunt Kinsley and I lived a hard life. You've enjoyed a cushy one. The first Lilly Day novel was a hit for a reason. It was raw." Lilly picked her coffee cup up, looking back at Kinsley. "Is there more?"

"Are you saying I can't be a great writer unless I'm raised homeless and killing roaches?" Enid asked.

As usual, Lilly turned to Kinsley for help but Kinsley remained quiet. She'd been reminding Lilly for two months now to read Enid's story. Lilly needed to step up and do so. Enid *did* have an exceptional voice that, with development, will be unparalleled.

High praise, sure, but Kinsley knew talent.

"Exactly what about my voice is unique?" Enid asked.

Delicately, Lilly cleared her throat.

"You didn't read it, did you?" Enid asked in a confrontational tone that surprised, and impressed, Kinsley.

"No, I haven't read it," Lilly admitted. "I've been busy."

"Then why not just say that?" Enid asked.

"Because I didn't want to hurt your feelings."

"*This* is hurting my feelings. I would rather you tell me you're busy than tell some national reporter I have a 'unique voice' when you don't even know that's true."

"Kinsley read it. She's the one who told me how talented you are."

"And yet you don't care," Enid snapped.

Lilly's mouth opened. So did Kinsley's. She'd never heard Enid talk back before.

Enid shook her head. "I'm going down to the pool." With that, she left the room.

Lilly sunk onto the edge of the bed. She didn't look at Kinsley. She simply stared at her lap.

Irritated on behalf of Enid, Kinsley folded her arms. She studied the crown of red hair on Lilly's head. Kinsley waited.

"What is wrong with me?" Lilly finally murmured.

Across the suite, Enid's flip-flops smacked hard on the wood floor. The door to the suite opened, then she slammed it so hard it shook the fixtures.

Lilly sighed.

Kinsley softened, just a little. She took the spot beside her sister. "Enid wants to be a writer. She craves your approval. It's not easy to be the daughter of Lilly Day."

"It's not easy to be the sister either." Lilly cut Kinsley a sardonic look.

"You have plenty of time in your schedule today," Kinsley said. "Read Enid's story. Then we'll chat. I'll help you put together notes."

"Okay. Thanks." Lilly put her head on Kinsley's shoulder. "I'm sorry about earlier."

"You screwed up."

"Yes. It won't happen again. I promise."

"You're allowed one screwup per week. That's yours for this week."

One screwup per week. That's a rule they made to keep Lilly in check. Otherwise, every moment of every day would be an ongoing issue.

"That way I don't become a narcissistic twat." Lilly repeated Kinsley's often used phrase for her.

A tiny smile played across Kinsley's lips. "Yes."

Lilly took Kinsley's hand. She fiddled with the ruby ring Kinsley always wore. "You need a break from being my long suffering sister. Why don't you go do something just for you today? I'll be fine. The girls will be fine. It'll give me a chance to give them some attention."

Kinsley liked this idea very much but she hesitated. Lilly didn't know how to behave herself without Kinsley constantly keeping her in check.

"Seriously." Lilly squeezed her hand. "Please go. Take some time just for you. I vow to watch my p's and q's," she promised, reading Kinsley's mind. "It'll be good for both of us."

CHAPTER 10

J anuary, Twenty-Eight Years Ago

Lilly did lose her scholarship.

She also lost the cash award.

The Wilkeses divorced.

Mrs. Wilkes told anyone who would listen that Lilly slept with her husband.

He lost his job at the university.

He moved to central Florida.

His ex-wife moved north to Georgia.

Lilly never saw either again.

After graduating high school, she went to work at a factory. She was awarded guardianship of me. We moved into a small apartment. I finished my sophomore year of high school, completed junior, and started my senior.

Mr. Young moved up each year that I did. Once again I had him as my teacher.

Now, On a frigid January day, I walk up three flights of exterior steps and let myself into our one-bedroom place.

With peeling paint, threadbare carpet, thin walls, and appliances that work when they want, I find Lilly sitting on our stained couch. Huddled over a yellow legal pad, she's furiously writing.

With a blanket over her shoulders, she glances up. "How was school?"

"Good."

"I bought *SpaghettiOs*."

My favorite. "Thanks."

"You're welcome." She goes back to writing.

"It's cold in here."

"Yes, it is."

Over at the wall, I check the thermostat. I flip the button from heat to off, and back to heat. I adjust the temperature. Nothing happens. "It's not working. Did you tell the manager?"

"No."

With a sigh, I walk into our bedroom with two twin mattresses on the floor. I place my book bag on my mattress. A roach scuttles across. "Did you buy roach motels?"

"No."

I let go of another sigh.

In the kitchen, I open a cabinet and get a pot. Another roach, this one bigger, scurries out. I slam it with the pot.

"Kinsley! Jesus, I'm working here."

I wipe the roach guts on my jeans and place the pot on the stove. From a cabinet higher up, I get the can of *SpaghettiOs*. Another roach slides past. I slam it with the can.

"Oh my God, what is your deal?"

With the can in my hand, I turn. One single bulb hanging in the center of the room casts my sister in an eerie white glow. "Today was your day off. You had one chore. *One*. Get rid of the roaches. Well, guess what? You didn't. Of course, you didn't! You also don't seem to mind our heat isn't working. It's freezing, Lilly."

She blinks.

I rarely, if ever, raise my voice.

A few tense seconds pulse by.

"But I bought *SpaghettiOs*," she says, like that even matters.

Another roach boldly appears next to the stove. I slam my fist down on it and wipe those guts on my jeans next to the others.

"I'm sorry. Okay? It's just, I had a great idea today for a novel." For proof, she holds up the legal pad. She thumbs through it. "I've nearly written my way through this entire pad." She shakes it. "This is the key, Kinsley. This will get us out of here. If I can do this in just one day, imagine what I can do if I had a whole week off. Imagine if I didn't work at all!"

I put the can down and leave.

Outside in the cold, I take the steps down to the ground floor. I pass the scent of cooking onions, the sound of a couple fighting, a crying baby, loud music, and the smell of pot.

People assume it does not get cold in Florida, but it does. I've heard it described as a wet cold—the kind that seeps into your bones. I've never been anywhere but Florida, but I get it because my bones do feel wet. I need a hot bath. But that would require a tub and hot water, neither of which we have.

I've never smoked or drank but I would try either if someone handed it to me.

I'd also love to kill another roach. There was something deeply satisfying about that.

Instead, I sit on the bottom step and I stare out at the parking lot filled with run-down vehicles. Not far from me, a drunk homeless man sleeps under a blanket that looks warmer than anything we own.

I can't believe how much money we pay for this place.

I'm not sure how much time goes by. I halfway expect my sister to come find me. But she doesn't. I halfway expect the homeless man to peek out at me and ask if I'm okay. But he doesn't. I halfway expect a knight in shining armor to make an appearance. But that doesn't happen either. Other than a car pulling up to let a woman out who walks off in the opposite direction, absolutely nothing happens.

I could stay here the rest of the afternoon and evening and nothing would happen. I almost do. But the hoodie I'm wearing insulates only so much. I do the only thing I can—I go to the manager's apartment and knock.

Wearing a stained tee, an overweight man appears. Warmth flows from his apartment, followed by the smell of something fried. I search my brain for the man's name but can't remember it. "Hi, my sister and I live in unit three-one-four. Our heat's out."

He holds up a finger before disappearing and coming back with a space heater. "Use this. I'm booked up today. I'll come by tomorrow."

"Got anything for roaches?"

Another finger goes up. He comes back with roach powder.

"Thanks."

"You're welcome." He shuts the door. I immediately miss the warmth.

Upstairs I walk back into our apartment. I'm already talking, "I've got a space heater and something for the roaches. The manager said he'd fix our thermostat tomorrow."

Lilly left the legal pad on the couch and with the blanket still over her shoulders she stands at our one grimy window, staring out at a cloudless sky. I come up beside her, now noting tears shimmering in her eyes.

They unsettle me. I can't recall ever seeing her cry. Of the two of us, she's the dramatic one, sure, but rarely if ever does her mood dip. She handles things with a determined toughness and can grin her way through pretty much any situation.

I touch her shoulder. "Lilly?"

"I hate our life."

"I know you do."

"I'm sorry I suck as a sister."

"You don't suck."

"Yes, I do." The tears spill out. Angrily, she wipes them away. "God."

"What's going to make you happy?"

She huffs a harsh laugh. "A new place to live."

"We'll start looking tomorrow."

"We can't afford a different place."

"Sure we can. We'll figure it out." I hug her. "What else will make you happy?"

"That's easy. Writing. Selling a novel. Becoming famous."

"Then write."

"How? I work six days a week at the factory. I'm exhausted when I get home. What, I'm supposed to write on my one day off *and* remember everything else?"

"What can I do?"

She sniffs. "I just need a year. That's all I need. One year to write my novel."

I take a breath. My thoughts spin. I walk over to the couch and pick up the legal pad. I flip through it, reading a sentence here, a paragraph there. She's silent as I do. Then I backtrack, more carefully studying the lines.

"You're writing about us." I note the title, *Sister Sister*.

"Yes."

"You need to cut the first five pages. It's backstory. You should work this in elsewhere."

She comes over. "You think so?"

"I do." I hand the pad to her. "Also, this should be a novel you write later in life. Our story is just beginning. You need more meat for a well-developed plot."

"Oh." She frowns. "Then what should I write about now?"

"What are your other ideas?"

"Um…none." She fiddles with the pad.

I think about the journals sitting in my locker that are part of Mr. Young's class. I think about all the short stories I've written for assignments. I'll gladly share my ideas with her if it makes her happy. "How about something of mine?"

Her face lights up. "You sure?"

"I am. In fact, this is what we're going to do. I'm going to see if I have enough credits to graduate early. If not, I'll drop out and get my GED. I'm going to ask my boss at KFC if I can go full time. If not there then somewhere else. Then, you're going to write."

She draws in a shocked breath. "Are you serious?"

"Very."

"Oh, Kinsley, I won't let you down." She hugs me hard. "I promise I won't waste this year. I'll make so much money you won't ever worry about anything again." Lilly releases me. "I'll make us *SpaghettiOs*." She spins an excited circle. "You know what else? One day this sorry-ass apartment will make a great story."

I walk into our bedroom. I sit on my mattress. From my book bag, I take out my latest journal and open it to Mr. Young's most recent note.

I suspect that many people will read your words.

CHAPTER 11

*arch, Present Day*

Despite Lilly promising all would be okay, Kinsley still printed her schedule, made notes in the margins, and touched base with the girls.

She felt free powering down her phone as she walked across the hotel lobby.

She felt free not having fans scrambling for pictures and autographs.

Free not having Julian hovering.

Free-free-free as she stepped out into the late morning sunshine.

She slid on sunglasses. She took her time strolling Rodeo Drive. She meandered in and out of stores, looking and enjoying.

Eventually, she found her way several blocks over to a quaint bookstore. She grabbed a coffee from the adjoining cafe and strolled the aisles. She bought two books—one a cozy mystery and another a historical thriller.

She didn't care how much time went by. Lately, there'd been no time to herself. She would savor every moment.

Back in the café, she sat at a small table situated in front of a cozy window. She ordered chicken Caesar salad. Halfway through the salad and several pages into the cozy mystery, she heard, "Kinsley Day?"

She glanced up. She froze. "M-Mr. Young?"

A good-natured chuckle bubbled up and out. "I think you can call me Niko now."

He stepped forward as she stood. They hugged. It had been nearly thirty years. Except for a receding hairline, he looked just the same—tall and strong, tan, light hair, and those green eyes that always seemed to glow.

"You haven't aged a bit," he said.

She rarely, if ever, got embarrassed. It took her off guard. "I wouldn't go that far, but thank you. *You* look exactly how I remember you."

"I came in for coffee. May I join you?"

"Of course."

Niko placed a book that he carried on her table before walking to the café counter. She quickly cleaned up her lunch mess, making room. She wanted a quick selfie peek with her phone but she didn't have time. He returned with a cup of drip coffee.

He sat. They stared at each other.

He laughed. She laughed.

"I seriously cannot believe it's you," he said.

"Ditto. What are you doing here?"

"I teach at UCLA. I love this bookstore. I come all the time." He blew his coffee, then sipped. "I assume you're here with Lilly?"

"Yes."

"Well, what have you been doing for the past three decades?"

"Not much, I suppose. My life is all about Lilly and my nieces."

"You never married?"

She took a sip of water. "No, never. You?"

"Yes, married briefly. We split amicably. We have a daughter. She's fifteen. They live here in LA."

Mr. Young with a teenage girl. Somehow that fit. "How long did you work at that horrible high school?" she asked.

"Not long. I stayed on about a year after I last saw you and then came out here for grad school and eventually accepted a faculty position." Niko sipped more coffee, studying her over the rim. "You never went to college?"

"No. I got my GED."

"I know you got your GED. One day you were at school and then poof, gone. You didn't even say goodbye."

"I'm sorry."

"It worried me."

"It did?"

"Of course. You were my one shining star in that school. I couldn't wait for Friday when I took up journals and got the chance to read yours. For that matter, anything you turned in I always waited until the end to grade it. Like a fabulous dessert after a subpar dinner."

Kinsley found herself speechless.

He sipped more of his warm drink, continuing to study her.

"You said you knew I got my GED?"

"Your sister told me."

"Excuse me?"

"I went to your apartment. Your sister told me you'd gotten your GED. From your response, I take it she never told you I dropped by."

"No, never."

"Ah."

Kinsley peered out the window. A few people strolled by.

It didn't surprise her that Lilly never told her. So predictable. Lilly spent ridiculous amounts of time flirting and charming Niko Young, but her overactive libido received no response. He showed up at their apartment asking for her little sister. It ruffled Lilly's ego.

A smirk snuck into Kinsley's lips. She hoped Lilly made all kinds of juicy wrong assumptions about his appearance at their apartment.

"What's that look about?" he asked, his tone amused.

"I want you to know that I looked forward to every Monday when I got my journal back from you. I would read and reread those little notes that you left me."

Folding his arms, Niko sat back in his chair. Kinsley boldly admired the stretch of the T-shirt covering his chest and biceps. She wanted him to know that her life may revolve around her sister but that did not make her a victim.

He said, "Will you come to my apartment with me? I have something that is going to shock the hell out of you."

CHAPTER 12

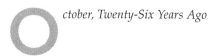ctober, *Twenty-Six Years Ago*

Lilly's one allotted year to write turned into two.

Other than taking one of my journal entries as an idea, she keeps her writing close. She doesn't want me to read it until it's finished, which she promises will be "any day now."

I only hope two years do not become three.

After a year of full time at KFC, I went to work at a hotel in downtown Jacksonville cleaning rooms. The upside to the job is that I get endless supplies of toiletry items. I also make tips plus one more dollar per hour.

This weekend the hotel's hosting a writer's conference. I stole a badge for Lilly. It's been four days of panel discussions, author signings, and various parties. She's gone to pretty much everything.

I hope she's learning something.

Dressed in my maid's uniform, I quietly slip into the back of the room hosting a Q&A with the headline author. I find my sister in a middle row of seating and slide into the empty chair beside her.

"Hi," she quietly says.

"Anything good?"

She makes a face.

Two chairs occupy the stage—one for the moderator and one for the author. Beside them, an easel displays a poster of the book cover.

I'd guess the author's pushing eighty with a cigarette voice and a look of sullenness about her. She's saying, "I ended up printing copies of my first book and selling them out of my trunk. I sold a hundred copies, most bought by family and friends."

Laughter scatters through the crowd. I don't know this author. Her cover is romance, though.

The moderator speaks, "You've been writing a long time now. 'Brilliant.' 'Vivid.' 'Bold.' These are all words used to describe your work."

"Once upon a time maybe." The author all but smirks. "No one cares about literary fiction from a woman. Maybe someday. But not now. All they think women can do is write romance." She shrugs. "Therefore, that's what I do."

An awkward beat goes by. The moderator shifts uncomfortably.

My sister leans in and mutters, "If I ever become bitter like that, shoot me."

The moderator clears her throat. "We have a lot of promising young writers in the audience. Any advice?"

"You want me to tell you to write every day and read widely. Sure, take that advice if you want. The truth, though? If you're a woman pick another career. You'll never be taken seriously. Men have always and will continue to dominate the field. Just look at any *New York Times* list. The same men hold the same slots every single week."

To my sister, I whisper, "Has the whole interview been like this?"

"Yeah."

"Well, we've reached our time." The moderator stands. "Let's give a round of applause…"

Softly, Lilly claps. "That's tragic and depressing." Around us, people gather their things and leave. "I'm going to catch a bus home. You still working?"

"I am. I'll be home around nine. I'm supposed to clean this room after it empties."

She gives me a quick hug and walks with the departing people through the exit. I sit for a few minutes, watching everyone leave and listening to their comments—most mirroring what Lilly said.

When the place empties, save for a young man and a middle-aged woman sitting up front, I begin stacking chairs. Another maid comes in to help me clean.

"Do we need to leave?" the young man asks me.

"No, you're fine."

To the woman, the young man says, "I can't find anyone. I read my slush piles religiously. I go to these conferences and sit through pitches. Nothing's jolting me. If I don't find something soon to represent, I'll need to resume my old job to make ends meet."

"It takes time, Julian. You can't expect a diamond to just appear. We all had to earn our stripes. It was five years before I landed my first solid author."

The young man, Julian, sighs.

I keep stacking chairs.

"I don't care what that old bag said, I want a talented woman writer. Preferably young and never published. I want to debut her and catapult her to the top. I don't even care what genre it is. Give me the talent and I'll form it into something great."

The woman laughs. "I hope that happens for you." She stands. "I have a meeting. We still on for drinks later?"

"You betcha."

The woman leaves. Julian wanders up to the stage. He stands, studying the easel with the poster cover still propped up.

I gather my courage and approach him.

———

That night, I let myself into our apartment. Lilly lays on the couch, a bowl of popcorn balanced on her stomach, watching our tiny black-and-white television. We didn't move apartments but we did get rid of the roaches, got our heating and air fixed, and acquired more used furniture.

I'm breathless and it has nothing to do with the three flights of stairs I just climbed. "Guess what?"

My sister glances up from the TV. "What?"

"After you left, I met this book agent. He's young. His name is Julian. I told him about the book you're writing and he wants to see it."

Lilly blinks. "Shut up."

"I'm serious."

The popcorn flies as she catapults herself from the couch. "When?"

"As soon as possible. He wants the first three chapters and a synopsis."

She grabs her head. "B-but it's not finished."

"It doesn't need to be finished. He said first three chapters."

"But you haven't even read it!"

"Well, give it to me."

"Is this for real?"

"Yes."

Lilly screams.

CHAPTER 13

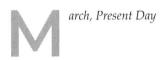*arch, Present Day*

They walked to where Niko parked his Bronco in a metered spot. He told her that he lived in Westwood, and as he drove, he talked nonstop about a recent trip he took to England with a few hand selected students. Kinsley tried so very hard to listen but was distracted by Niko Young, her high school English teacher, who—though she would have never admitted it back then—she had (and probably still did) a crush on.

Eventually, they pulled alongside a curb and parked. They walked into a U-shaped courtyard bracketed by two floors of apartments. He led her up to the second floor and into a two-bedroom apartment decorated with masculine vintage pieces.

Shelves lined every available wall, neatly stacked with books. Kinsley's focus fell on a row of Lilly Day novels. Her mood soured.

Until she noticed her high school journals—eight yellow

ones in all—there on the shelf above the Lilly Day published works.

She inhaled a sharp breath.

Niko had been busy saying hi to his cat. He straightened when he heard her. "Ah, shoot. I didn't want you to see those yet." He moved across the hardwood floor, carefully sliding each one from its slot.

She remained standing at the entrance, watching him, surrounded by the faint smell of laundry detergent and lemon. Her feet finally moved forward. She sat on his rich brown leather couch. He took the cushion beside her, still holding the journals.

"I can't believe you have those. But how?"

"You came to school on a Friday and never returned. I saw the janitor cleaning your locker. I asked for the journals. I've carried them around since then." Niko slid them over onto her lap. "They are yours now."

She stared down at them, unable to fully grasp what she held. Lightly her fingers rested on the top one. Her confused gaze met his. "But why?"

"Because, Kinsley, you are and have always been the most talented writer I've ever had the privilege of teaching. I couldn't bear to see your words get thrown into a garbage can."

Kinsley felt unable to process this.

His hand came to rest on top of hers. "Please tell me you kept writing."

To that she made no response.

Something unspoken passed between them. Like he was disappointed in her unused potential. Or he held these high expectations that were never met. Or something else…

The whole thing irritated her. "I haven't taken a backseat to my sister. If that's what you're thinking."

His hand squeezed hers before releasing.

Why she kept talking, she couldn't say. Kinsley never overexplained anything. "I don't have the personality to be some world famous author. I'm way too introverted. You should see how Lilly works with the crowds. I would never survive. I hate being the center of attention. I can't stand it when people look at me."

"I'm looking at you."

She fell quiet.

Carefully, Niko studied her.

Her hands grew clammy. He unsettled her. She didn't like that. At all.

He stood. "Wine?"

"Please."

He moved away. She breathed.

Kinsley placed the journals on the matching leather ottoman. She itched to look at them, yet she also never wanted to see them again.

She followed Niko, coming to stand at the island that separated the kitchen from the living room. Niko uncorked the white wine that he took from the refrigerator.

He said, "You've had your work cut out for you with Lilly, I'm sure. She doesn't seem very low maintenance."

"No, low maintenance is not in her vocabulary. In fact, she says she has a compulsive disorder to mess up her life."

Niko poured the wine into two glasses. "Maybe you have a compulsive disorder to fix her life."

So very true.

He handed her a glass. They toasted. They sipped. For several silent beats, he contemplated her.

"What?" she asked.

"You, dear Kinsley, have always been and still are quite the lovely mystery."

Something in her shifted. Like this shy teenage girl who grew into an introverted adult suddenly became fired up with a woman she didn't recognize.

The next words that came from her mouth were more Lilly than Kinsley. "Are you flirting with me, Mr. Young?"

"Yes. I believe I am."

She loved that response.

Slowly, Niko rotated his glass. "I have a confession."

"Do tell." Her pulse quickened.

"I've devoted my life to teaching. For the most part, I've loved every day. I love when students surprise me. It's very rare though that I'm moved. *You*, Kinsley, moved me the first day I met you. You were this shy, brave beautiful girl dying to make a mark. I suspected before I even read your words that you would be a great writer. You had that soulful look about you. I saw you once. I came to one of Lilly's signings here in LA. In truth, I went hoping to see you. And there you were standing with lovely poise."

"Why didn't you say hi?" she asked.

"I tried to catch your eye, but there were so many people. I stayed for an hour, then ended up leaving as I had a class to teach. I wish now I would've skipped that class."

She loved his words. She loved that story.

She felt giddy.

He peered at her, waiting for her to speak. But she didn't know what to say. Instead, she allowed her gaze to touch his strong jaw, the lines on his forehead, and his manly lips.

"Where does your genius come from?" he quietly asked.

Kinsley didn't want to talk anymore.

She walked around the island, coming to a stop in front of him. Their eyes met. She came up on her tiptoes at the same time he tilted forward. Their breaths mingled.

Their lips touched.

CHAPTER 14

January, Twenty-Five Years Ago

After a full work day plus several hours of overtime cleaning hotel rooms, I let myself into our apartment.

I'm in the middle of a yawn when Lilly gets into my face. "Where've you been?"

"Work, where do you think?" I push past her, going straight into our bedroom.

"I finished the book. But I don't want to send it to Julian until you read it."

My eyes feel heavy. I wrestle with the zipper on the back of my uniform. "I read the first few chapters and helped you with those. Isn't that enough?"

"And those are the chapters that made Julian request the whole thing." She brushes my fingers away and unzips me. "Please, Kinsley. *Please.* I can't send him the entire manuscript without you reviewing it. Think about my fragile writer's ego."

I wedge off my tennis shoes. I roll the hose down my legs. I stifle another yawn. "When?"

Lilly picks up my stuff. She holds my dirty clothes to her chest. "He wants it by the end of the week."

I blink. "That's two days from now!"

She winces. "I'll make you coffee. Run you a bath. Give you a massage. I'll do all the cleaning for a whole month. Make you dinner every night. I'll—"

I hold up a hand. "Fine." I walk past her and into the bathroom. "Did you already print it? I hate computer screens."

"Yes, at the library." Following behind me, she turns on the shower for me.

"Give me ten minutes, then I'll be ready."

Loudly, she kisses me. "Oh, thank you. Thank you. Thank you. Thank you."

———

I stay up all night reading. On her mattress in our shared room, Lilly sleeps soundly.

Quietly, I go into the kitchen. I make myself a new pot of coffee. As I wait for it to brew I walk over to the dingy window overlooking the dark and empty alley three stories below.

Groggily, Lilly comes from the bedroom. "Are you done?"

"Yes."

"And?"

I have no words. She took my idea plus all the work I did on the first chapters and ruined the rest. Julian will not like this.

"What?" Lilly moves closer.

I turn to face her. Carefully, I choose my words. "It needs… work."

She frowns. "What do you mean?"

"The first few chapters are stellar. After that…"

Lilly scowls. "The first few chapters are stellar? Those are the ones you helped me with."

"No, those are the ones I completely rewrote. Let's be honest."

"So, I'm a crap writer?"

I sigh.

"Well, way to buffer the criticism, *sis*." She folds her arms. "What's wrong with it?"

"It's flat. Nothing jumps out at me. It's like reading a summary with way too many passive phrases. As a reader, I'm not in the book at all. I'm not invested. This is the story of a young woman growing up alone with a disabled elderly lady as her guardian. It's haunting and tragic. Sensitive and heartbreaking. It's lyrical. At least that's what it's supposed to be."

Lilly scoffs. "It was your idea!"

"But not like this."

"You're too close to the subject matter. That's the problem."

No, you butchered it. That's the problem.

"You didn't even graduate high school. I'm the one who won an essay contest, not you. I'm the one—"

"You won that contest because I rewrote the entire thing. You might as well be honest about that too. Technically that means *I* won the contest. And do I really need to remind you that you're the reason I didn't graduate high school?"

Her mouth snaps shut. She seethes. "What're you trying to tell me? Do you want to be the writer in the family? Do you want to quit your job so you can write?" She throws her hands up. "Fine. Whatever. I'll give up my dream. I'm sure I can get that horrible job back at the factory."

She takes the manuscript from where I left it on the coffee table and stomps back into our bedroom. She yells, "I'm getting a second opinion."

I take a breath. In the kitchen, I pour a cup of coffee. I check the time. In two hours I clock in for my shift.

Through the open bedroom door, I watch Lilly look at the manuscript. Her gaze bounces across the pages. Her jaw clenches. She balls up the first page and throws it. She does the same with the second. The third. She grabs giant sections and hurls them. Then she begins tearing.

Calmly, I walk over to the couch and sit down.

She flounces from the bedroom. "You and me living together? It's not working."

"Well, considering I pay all the bills, what are you going to do?"

She screams.

She disappears back into the bedroom. I listen to her continue ripping the pages. I sip my coffee.

She reappears, holding up a ball of paper. "If you thought my writing sucked, why didn't you tell me sooner."

"Because of this. You can't take the truth. You're a giant brat."

"Up yours!"

"Classic."

She jabs a finger in my direction. "You don't believe in me. You don't believe in us. You never have."

"Is that why I got my GED and took on a full-time job—because I don't believe in you?"

"You only did those things because I asked."

"Yes. But also because you're all I have in this world. Despite your high maintenance dramatics, I do want you happy."

"Screw this." Lilly stomps back into the bedroom. "I'm done."

I sip my coffee. I check the time. I wait for her to make another histrionic entrance, but none come. It's unusually quiet.

I find her face down on her mattress.

Of course.

I sit down beside her.

"What am I going to do?" she murmurs. "It's not like I can sleep my way to the top. Julian's gay."

"True."

"I can't go back to work at the factory." She grabs my hand and tucks it under her face. "I just can't."

"You can take creative writing classes. You can try again later with the novel. It's not going anywhere."

"But that'll take forever," she whines.

"Not so long."

"How come you're so naturally talented? I'm the one who wants to be a writer. You don't even care."

Yet, I do care. However, when I write it's just for me. I don't need the fame and fortune she so desperately desires.

"I want to be a literary sensation. That's all I've ever wanted. But now, nothing. I'll never see my name in a bookstore. I'll never get a movie deal. I'll never autograph books. I'll be a bitter and angry old woman. Just like that one we saw at the writer's conference."

Despite her temper tantrum, she seems calmer now. I extract my hand from under her cheek. I move her hair from her face. She scoots over to lay her head on my lap. I comb my fingers through her hair. Her eyes close. I rub slow circles on her back.

"Don't ever leave me," she whispers. "I'm sorry I said that earlier. I don't want to live alone."

"I know."

"Promise?"

"I promise."

"Really, Kinsley. What am I going to do?"

"I believe it's more what am *I* going to do?"

Her eyelids snap open. "What do you mean?"

"I'm going to call in sick to work. I'm going to keep those first chapters I reworked and ditch the rest. I'm going to write an entirely new novel for you. Meanwhile, you're going to contact Julian and ask if the end of next week is okay for a delivery date."

She sits up. She stares at me, confused. "You're going to write a whole novel for me?"

"Just this once."

"Can't you help me rewrite what I already did?"

"That'll take way too much time. I'd rather work from scratch." I stand. "It's this way or nothing."

"But..." She thinks about things for a few seconds. "Just this once?"

I nod. "If he likes it, signs you as an author, and sells the book, then you need to be ready to write future books. Okay?"

"Absolutely." A slow grin curves her face. "Are you sure?"

"Yes."

"Okay, just this once. We'll split whatever money we make."

"You mean whatever money *I* make?"

She rolls her eyes. "You know what I meant."

"Yes, of course."

She takes my hand. "You hate computers. How about you dictate and I'll type. Or you can handwrite and I'll transcribe. Whatever. At least then I'll be contributing."

"Okay, deal."

I turn to leave as she asks, "What do you want in return?"

"I'll let you know when I figure that out."

CHAPTER 15

arch, Present Day

Niko and Kinsley's kiss led to more.

So much more.

Despite Lilly's assumptions about Kinsley's sex life, she led a healthy one—the details of which were none of her sister's business.

She'd had several one night stands, never once regretting them. She also kept a few *friends with benefits* when the mood struck. Did she want more? Once upon a time maybe, but like so many other things, Lilly ruined that too.

Niko's lips were currently doing all kinds of magical things along her neck. "Luscious. Delicious. Delightful. Lovely. Beautiful. Gorgeous. St—"

She chuckled. "What are you doing?"

"Listing all the words that come to mind when I think of you and what we just did. Two times." Niko nuzzled her ear.

Lazily, her fingers played across his back.

"Stunning. Splendid. Spectacular. Marvelous. Wonde—"

"Stop already." Playfully she nudged him.

He slid off of her to prop himself up on a hand. He trailed a languid finger over the planes of her face. "You and Lilly look nothing alike."

"Most people say we do."

"I mean, same features, but the emotion through your face, the depth in your eyes, the intellect in that brain of yours —it makes you look so very different."

She rolled to face him. "Are you saying my sister has no complexity or wit?"

"From what I remember of her, no."

Kinsley loved that response.

He fiddled with the ends of her shoulder-length hair. "I gotta tell you, if you had come onto me as your sister did, I probably would've gotten into trouble—one of those tragic stories where the teacher hooks up with a student."

"You are lying."

"I am not." He pressed a kiss to her forehead. "What's inside here intrigued me." He tapped her heart. "But what's inside here stirred me. It still does."

Like so many other times in the past several hours, she found herself without words.

"You've yet to confess what you thought of me back then," he said.

"Oh, I had a crush on you, for sure. If I could tell the younger me what just happened, I'd probably stroke out."

"And now?"

"Still stroking."

They shared a laugh.

Kinsley couldn't recall the last time she felt so comfortable. This was a man she hadn't seen in almost thirty years, yet no awkwardness existed.

Their hands intertwined. A long moment went by while he caressed his finger up and down each of hers.

Gradually though, something shifted. His prior amusement faded. His after sex glow dimmed. His brows drew together. He broke eye contact as he fiddled again with her hair.

Then his hand trailed down to caress the faded horizontal scar on her lower abdomen. Kinsley would tell him about that scar if he wanted to know.

She waited.

He took a deep breath. His eyes once again met hers. "I want to ask you something but I don't know how."

"Just ask."

"I've read all of Lilly's novels. I've read all of your journals." He stopped talking.

This was not the question she expected. She waited for him to continue but he didn't.

"And?" she prompted.

"And…the writing…well… it seems similar."

"We are sisters. We share the same talent. Also, I'm her first reader. I make suggestions. Naturally, my voice blends with her."

Niko contemplated her. "It seems to me you do more than make suggestions."

"I'm not sure what you're getting at." Naked, she sat up. Though she didn't care about the time, she still looked at the clock on his nightstand. "I have to go."

"You're wasting your talent."

She ignored him. In his bathroom, she made quick work of redressing. When she emerged Niko stood fully clothed holding his keys.

"I'll drive you."

"That's okay, I'll take an Uber." She found her purse and dug out her phone.

"Kinsley."

"I really do have to go."

"I'm sorry. Please don't leave. Stay and talk to me. You can trust me."

She made a hasty exit.

Back at the hotel, she realized that she left her high school journals on his ottoman.

CHAPTER 16

*F*ebruary, Twenty-Two Years Ago

Roughly three years after Lilly emailed Julian the finished manuscript, the novel debuted, hitting number one on the *New York Times* Best Sellers list.

During those three years, a lot happened.

We bought a condo.

I quit my job at the hotel.

I became Lilly's "assistant."

Work began on a second book.

A deal was signed for a third.

"Just this once" turned into twice.

The first book was optioned for a movie.

I also began dating Asher Hill. Asher worked as an accountant at the firm we hired to handle our taxes. I was there delivering paperwork when I met him. We—as people say—just clicked. At twenty-seven he was three years older than me. Though I never imagined myself falling for someone, I fell hard for Asher.

Today we're celebrating our three-month anniversary.

"I love that you did a picnic for us." He kisses my cheek.

I'm not a romantic type of girl, but picnics and soft kisses, cuddling, and surprise presents seem to be part of my life now. Yeah, Asher brings something out in me.

I let us into the two-bedroom condo that I own with Lilly. She sits at the corner desk, staring at the screen as her fingers move over the keyboard.

I freeze. "What are you doing?"

She jumps. "I-I didn't hear you come in."

"*What* are you doing?"

"Nothing." Nervously, she laughs. "Reworking a scene that's all."

My jaw tightens.

She notices the shift in me and quickly stands.

For several seconds we stare at each other.

Asher clears his throat. "I'll wait in your bedroom."

I listen to his feet tread the hallway toward my room. I move across the living room to Lilly. She backs away. I sit down and read the screen. My hand lands on the mouse. I scroll up. I scroll down. If smoke really could blow out of my ears, it would be erupting from mine.

"I'm sorry," she whines. "I had a great idea for that scene. I wanted to get it done before you got home."

I click on the folder labeled "Novels." I search for a past saved version. I can't find it. I go to the trash. It's empty. My fingers grab the corners of the desk. The muscles in my arms, my shoulders, and my neck tense as I tightly squeeze.

"It's my name, Kinsley. I want to do something other than just transcribe."

My words come measured. "Where is the saved version?"

"Will you at least read what I wrote?"

"Where is the saved version?"

Lilly sighs. "I'll get it."

She disappears down a hallway that leads to her room.

She comes back carrying the printed version. She stops a few feet from the desk. "I have to retype it. I permanently deleted it."

"*Why* would you do that?"

"So you'd be forced to read what I wrote."

I yank the manuscript from her hands. "I'll retype it. I don't trust you."

"Kinsley—"

"Tomorrow's the deadline."

"I know."

"You know? That's the worst response ever. How could you, Lilly? This was perfect. It was ready. Now it's trash."

Her jaw drops.

"Leave me alone." I ignore her as I flip through the manuscript, find the deleted scene, and begin retyping it.

Lilly's voice comes soft. "That's not the only scene I reworked."

I see red.

"I circled the page numbers that I rewrote." With that, Lilly turns and walks from the living room. "You could at least read what I did," she murmurs.

——————

I sit at the computer for hours, retyping the horror she made of my priceless art. For every minute that ticks by I don't regain my calm. No, I fume.

By the time I finish and click save, something dark and oily has festered in my soul. I want Lilly to suffer the consequences.

I go to her room.

For a long moment I stand beside her bed, my fists clenched, watching her sleep. Every peaceful breath she takes, my nails dig deeper into my palms. I've been out there in the living room typing for hours and here she is sound asleep like she doesn't care that our whole lives revolve around her.

I should let her fail. I should claim ownership.

But I can't. My voice is too wrapped up and known as Lilly Day. If I branched out on my own I'd have to do it under a pseudonym. Readers would quickly detect the same voice. The truth is I've doomed myself and in order for me to write I must remain channeled through Lilly.

I lose it.

I smack her across the face. She wakes with a startled gasp. She scrambles up in bed. In the dark of her room, I loom over her, jabbing a finger in her face. "You asked me one time what I want for all that I sacrifice? Well, this is it. I want to hurt you!" I slap her again.

Then, I leave.

Outside in the living room, I stand for several minutes, unable to believe what I just did. Yet also experiencing… relief, control, power.

I love the way I feel.

It's after one in the morning when I finally walk into my bedroom and find Asher fully clothed and asleep on top of the white down comforter. He still even wears his glasses. I take them off and set them aside. After slipping into the lingerie I bought, I try to wake him to no avail. Instead, I slide under the covers and into sleep…

I'm not sure what wakes me, but my eyes fly open. Disoriented I stare at the unmoving ceiling fan before glancing at the bedside clock that reads 4:23 in the morning.

Asher is gone.

After sliding a long T-shirt on over my lingerie, I exit the bedroom. Down the hall in the kitchen, I see an uncorked bottle of white wine on the counter. That wasn't there when I went to bed.

A light flickers through the otherwise dark room, indicating the TV is on. I don't hear it though. Instead, I hear Asher's quiet words, "Lilly, this is beautiful."

Her voice comes breathless. "You truly think so?"

"I do. Your talent is nothing less than marvelous."

My footsteps are soft as I walk the hall, coming to stand at the corner where I now see my sister and my boyfriend inches from each other on the brand new yellow couch. Two almost empty wine glasses sit on the light wood coffee table. With disheveled dark hair and his glasses back on, Asher holds the printed pages of the finished manuscript. My sister leans in, looking at the paragraph he's currently reading.

He glances up.

Their eyes meet.

A beat goes by.

His gaze roams her face, touching her brow, cheeks, and nose, before stopping on her lips.

She licks them.

He swallows.

A tiny grin curves her cheeks.

Slowly, Asher leans in.

It's then he notices that I'm watching and jerks back, standing. "Kinsley, did we wake you?"

Quickly, my sister picks up the wine glasses and walks them into the kitchen.

Asher places the printed pages on the couch. "I couldn't sleep. I came out for a snack. Lilly was gracious enough to let me read her latest work." He walks to me, holding out a hand. "Let's go back to bed."

My sister ignores me as she corks the wine and puts it in the refrigerator.

Asher tugs me down the hall. I allow him to. In my room, he starts nuzzling my neck, but I turn away.

Later, when he's back to sleep I lay wide awake thinking about all the times my sister tagged along with us on our outings. All the times Asher innocently suggested we invite her.

I think about them laughing and sharing a beer while the three of us were bowling.

About them giggling while we flew kites.

Whispering in the movie theater.

Playfully shoving each other during a game of pool.

Rolling around on the beach fighting over a giant conch shell.

Screaming their heads off on a roller coaster.

Linking pinkies and skipping across a park.

Getting into a water fight at our condominium's pool.

I was pleased my sister and boyfriend were getting along. But now I see the connection between them that I didn't notice before. The thing is, I don't like beer. Kite flying bores me. I hate people who talk in movies. I'm no good at pool. I would never roll around on the beach because I don't want sand where it shouldn't be. Roller coasters make me sick. I'm not a girl who skips. While I like water, I'm no good at swimming.

Blinded by love. I've heard that phrase. I just never thought it would apply to me. Asher and Lilly… naïve of me, yes, but more like stupid.

I am not a woman who lacks intelligence. But I am a woman who struggles to connect with her emotional side. Perhaps that's why I like to write. It gets my thoughts out without me having to speak them or show them.

Picnics and soft kisses, cuddling, and surprise presents? I made something out of nothing. In truth, it had been one picnic. A soft kiss came rarely. We'd cuddled twice, sort of. We'd had sex exactly three times—all initiated by me. Only one surprise present had been given—a book from him to me —where I acted as if I enjoyed it. In truth, the book uninterested me. And the way his eyes roamed her face as he drank in her features? He's never once done that with me.

My boyfriend doesn't come around here for me. We didn't "click." We shared a chuckle over something I said and I mistook that for clicking. The truth is, he likes my sister, and she likes him back.

But it's *my* writing he considers marvelous. Not Lilly's. Mine.

CHAPTER 17

arch, *Present Day*

Niko's questions left Kinsley unsteady.

When she walked back into the hotel suite, she expected to be bombarded by Lilly, the girls, Julian, whoever... but all appeared normal.

She didn't like that. She needed to control the chaos that constantly surrounded her sister. It would help Kinsley focus.

Stretched out on the sofa, Tessa wore earphones as she laughed at something on her iPad. The sound of soft voices drew Kinsley to Lilly's room. Enid sat beside her mother at the desk. Leaning close, Enid listened carefully as Lilly pointed a few things out on the printed pages of her daughter's novella. Enid's face glowed under Lilly's attention.

An unreasonable twinge of jealousy moved through Kinsley. Wasn't this what she wanted, though—for Lilly to pay more attention to Enid? But what did Lilly even know? Kinsley was the writer in the family, not Lilly.

Lilly's saying, "Kinsley's right. You've got a gift."

Enid tried not to let her already giant smile grow bigger. But it came anyway. "Thank you."

"You've got your story arc in place. For a short submission, the characters are well developed. Your choice of words has the maturity of someone much older."

Enid faltered. "I sense a but in here."

"But the story of sisters—one good and one bad—is cliché. One is stoic. The other is vibrant. You've got repressed rage. Selfishness. There's a double-crossing. It's been done too much. You would need a twist to make the story stand out."

"What kind of twist?"

"Well, that's for you to determine, now isn't it?" Lilly paused, taking in her daughter's rejected face. "All first drafts are just that—a first draft. Put this one away and start brainstorming another. Or think about that twist. Come up with a few ideas and we'll look at them together."

"Really?"

"Absolutely."

"Okay." Enid took a few seconds to straighten the pages. "How do you do it?"

"Do what?"

"Develop so many unique ideas."

"I don't know. I just do."

"It's too much work," she mumbled, almost painfully. "Is it worth it?"

Lilly stared at Enid, apparently formulating a response.

But one didn't come.

Kinsley stepped in. "I'm back. You probably should leave for your scheduled dinner. You don't want to be late."

Lilly didn't move. She kept staring at Enid.

Kinsley cleared her throat. She retrieved Lilly's purse from the bed and held it out. "Lilly?"

Her sister had no choice but to do as she was told.

CHAPTER 18

arch, *Twenty-One Years Ago*

On stage sits a panel of speakers—all *New York Times* bestselling authors—four total, with Lilly, at twenty-seven, being the youngest and the only woman.

A television crew busies itself doing last minute things. Several assistants stand around, watching the famous writers in awe. The three male authors chat amicably with the morning show reporter. A round coffee table prominently displays a selected hardcover novel from each guest. For Lilly, it's her second published book and the one she almost ruined.

My sister sits in the last chair glancing around the studio. She's been interviewed before but never with other authors more well-known than her. She's hiding it well, but she's intimidated by their talent and intelligence.

Good, she should be.

Beside me stands Julian. He leans in. "What is she doing?"

"She's nervous."

"Should I go talk to her?"

"If you want."

Julian checks the time. "We've only got five minutes." He hurries past the cameras and up onto the stage. The female reporter and the three other authors pause in their lively discussion. Lilly casts Julian a relieved look. He leans down and whispers something into her ear.

With a nod, she gently pushes him away.

"Everything okay?" the reporter asks.

Lilly plants a big fake grin on her face and to the other authors says, "I'm Lilly Day by the way."

The three men share a confused, amused glance.

The reporter says, "We…know that."

This earns a chuckle from the others, including the cameramen.

Lilly keeps that grin frozen in place. I can tell she's searching for something witty to rebuttal, but coming up blank.

The reporter and authors keep staring at her when the producer steps up onto the stage. He makes a quick visual sweep of the writers. "Everyone good with the questions?"

Heads nod.

To me, Julian whispers, "Questions? What questions?"

I shrug.

Lilly sees that shrug and her eyes widen. "Um." Her hand goes up. "What questions?"

"The questions we sent your team." The producer checks his clipboard.

"I'm sorry." Lilly glances at the producer. "We didn't get any questions."

The author sitting beside her says, "It's standard stuff. Don't worry about it."

"Oh, I see." My sister bristles. "You all get a chance to prepare ahead of time and I don't?"

An awkward beat goes by.

The reporter says, "Tell you what, I'll make sure you go

last with all the *hard* questions. That way you have time to formulate responses. Does that make you feel better?"

"No, it doesn't make me feel better."

The producer steps off stage. "We're out of time. Just do your best."

"In five. Four. Three…"

Even from my spot across the studio, I sense her nerves.

The camera rolls. My sister centers herself. The reporter makes introductory remarks, then she directs her first *hard* question at Lilly.

"Oh, no," Julian murmurs.

Has it been a year since Asher and I broke up? Sure.

Did he and Lilly come to me last week and ask permission to date? You betcha.

Is this even about Asher? Not really.

Did I receive and throw away the interview questions? Of course.

Is it juvenile of me? Yep.

Does it fill me with evil joy that Lilly's currently bombing the interview? Oh yes, very much so.

———

After the interview, Lilly comes straight toward me. Her lips barely move. "We even?"

"With Asher? Sure, why not."

"And everything else?"

"Nowhere near."

CHAPTER 19

arch, Present Day

Lilly and Kinsley dressed in evening gowns, ready for the Oscars. They were both in blue—Lilly's vibrant and Kinsley's pale—complementing their features.

In her room, Kinsley stood in front of the mirror, staring at her reflection. Niko's long ago journal comments floated through her mind…

> *I love the shape of your stories.*
> *Promise me you'll keep writing.*
> *I suspect that many people will read your words.*

"I am so nervous." Lilly swooshed in. She took one look at Kinsley and frowned. "That's how you're wearing your hair? But we decided that you'd wear it up because I *have* to wear mine down."

"My hair is fine."

Lilly folded her arms. "You can't wear it like that."

Kinsley turned away from the mirror. She took an intimidating step forward. Her eyes narrowed. "Yes, I can. And I will."

"Jeez." Lilly held her hands up. "Fine. Whatever."

Kinsley's fingers tightened into two fists.

Lilly noted them. She stepped back.

On the other side of the suite, the doorbell sounded.

"Th-that must be Julian," Lilly said.

"I'll get it!" Tessa yelled.

A few seconds later Julian entered Kinsley's room, dressed in a tux, and carrying a canvas grocery bag.

Lilly shook out her hair. Turning all of her attention onto Julian, she twirled. "How do we look?"

"Mind giving us a minute?" he said to Tessa.

With a nod, she closed the door.

The mood in the room became weighted. Julian, usually exuberant and loud, didn't say a word. He simply held the canvas bag as he glanced between them.

"What?" Lilly asked. "We're supposed to be downstairs in a few minutes. Our limo is waiting."

Julian walked over to the queen size bed and upended the canvas bag. Out tumbled Kinsley's high school journals.

"What are those?" Lilly asked.

Julian said, "This morning I checked messages at the front desk. These had just been dropped off for Kinsley. I told the receptionist I would get them to you."

"What are they?" Lilly repeated.

"My high school journals." Kinsley's voice came matter of fact. "I ran into Mr. Young yesterday. I'm sure you remember him. My high school English teacher?"

"Of course, I remember Mr. Young. Why didn't you tell me?"

Julian said, "You were out this morning, so I took them to my room. I'll admit to being nosy. I thumbed through—"

"Those are private," Kinsley said.

"And?" Lilly's brows went up.

Lilly never knew about Kinsley's journals. Kinsley kept them private—just between her and Mr. Young.

Julian picked one up. He flipped through the pages. He pointed to the margins. He handed that to Lilly. He picked up another, flipping through, pointing to the margins, and handing that one to Kinsley. He picked up another, this one holding. "Your Mr. Young has expertly notated how Kinsley's journals exactly match up to Lilly's writing."

"This is absurd." Lilly slammed hers closed. She flung it onto the bed.

"Please tell me you two haven't pulled off the biggest publishing fraud in history."

"Don't be an idiot." Lilly slid past him.

Julian followed. "Set me straight then."

"There's nothing to set straight." Lilly rushed across the suite and into her room. She came back out carrying a handbag. "Kinsley, let's go!"

Carefully, Kinsley collected the journals and placed them back inside the canvas bag.

Tessa and Enid were in the kitchen putting together a buffet of junk food, ready to watch the Oscars.

"What's going on?" Tessa asked.

"Nothing's going on." Lilly glared at Julian, silently telling him to get out.

He didn't move.

"Mom?" Enid hesitantly asked.

With steady steps, Kinsley crossed the suite to where Julian stood. She put a firm hand on his shoulder. "Its best if you get your own ride. We'll see you at the after-party."

———

In the limo Lilly and Kinsley sat across from each other. Lilly stared at Kinsley while Kinsley stared out the window as Beverly Hills rolled by.

"What are we going to do?" Lilly asked.

"You are going to do what you do best. Grin, work the crowd, and be Lilly Day. I am going to do what I do best, figure this out." Kinsley's shrewd gaze penetrated Lilly's nervous one. "Now be quiet. I need to think."

CHAPTER 20

ay, *Fourteen Years Ago*

With a hand on my third-trimester swollen belly, I let myself into Lilly and Asher's home. I walked here from my condo. It's only a half mile and I wanted the exercise. Plus, it's too pretty outside to drive.

In the home office, our desks sit on opposing walls. When Asher's around, we close the door.

I power up my laptop. I hate computers but I seem to use one more and more as the years wear on.

On my desk sit yesterday's printed pages. I need to read through them before I start writing today's word count that'll finally take me to the end of book four. It's hard to believe it's been eight years since book number one was written. Ideally, I'd like to do one per year but I'm not as fast of a writer as I used to be. Lilly complains I'm too much of a perfectionist. Yeah, well, my attention to detail is paying off.

With most every book debuting at number one on the *New York Times* list, each outselling the last, foreign translation deals, garnering various awards and film adaptations, my success has more than proved I know what I'm doing.

I no longer allow my sister anywhere near my work in progress. I don't trust her. Hell, I even put a password on my computer to make sure. No, in here she earns her keep by being my assistant and out there she's the face of Lilly Day.

While the laptop comes to life I walk across the tile floor into the kitchen where I pour myself a tall glass of filtered water. My breaths come heavier than usual. I sit at the kitchen table, propping my feet on a nearby chair. I left my lumbar pillow in the chair beside me when I was here yesterday. I stuff it behind my lower back.

As I drink water, I take deep breaths and stare out at the palm tree lined lanai.

From across the house, voices filter from Asher and Lilly's room.

Asher: "Where were you last night?"

Lilly: "Out. I told you I was out."

Asher: "You got home at two in the morning."

Lilly: "So."

Asher: "I was worried sick."

Lilly: "I'm a big girl."

Silence.

Lilly: "What?"

Asher: "Don't do this to me again."

Lilly: "Do what?"

Silence.

Lilly: "Why don't you spell it out for me."

Asher: "You came home smelling like booze and sex."

Lilly: "Oh please."

Asher: "What is wrong with you?"

Lilly: "Nothing."

Silence.

Asher: "Ever since your last miscarriage you've been uncontrollable. You're drinking at all hours. You're smoking.

You leave for days on end. You're spending money faster than you make it. Hell, I'm surprised you've managed to make your deadlines. I've tried to be supportive but, dammit Lilly, snap out of it."

Lilly: "'Snap out of it?' You don't know shit."

Asher: "I know your sister is carrying our daughter. That there's a beautiful nursery just waiting. And that we're going to be parents very soon."

Lilly: "Yeah, well, what if I've changed my mind?"

Asher: "About being a mom? News flash, it's a little late."

Lilly: "Kinsley can keep the baby. I don't want her."

Asher: "Don't say that."

Lilly: "I need space. Don't follow me."

Her bare feet slap against the tile as she crosses through the house. I stay where I am at the kitchen table watching the hallway for her appearance. She erupts through the archway only half dressed in a bra and shorts. She comes up short when she sees me.

I don't speak.

Lilly stomps into the kitchen and pours a cup of coffee. She opens a box of donuts on the counter and selects an apple fritter. She stands there drinking coffee, eating the fritter, and pretending like I'm not sitting here.

Lilly and Asher eloped six months into dating. Though they've never said, I suspect they eloped to be sensitive to me. They didn't need to. I've been over Asher a very long time.

Six months into the marriage, they began trying for a baby. For a woman who said she never wanted children, Lilly became obsessed with the idea.

"I need something all mine," she whined. "You won't let me do anything anymore. It's always about what you want. I need this, Kinsley. I need a child."

Though I was used to her dramatics, something about her tone had tugged at me. Despite all the sacrifices I had made for my sister, I did want Lilly happy.

Her gradual decline had been hard to see. Miscarriages. Fertility treatments. Emergency room visits. Many a night I held her while she sobbed. Then at the age of thirty-four came her hysterectomy. I had to do something. She was barely able to function.

I volunteered to be their surrogate.

When I told her, something in her lit up. I saw a glimpse of the old Lilly. I had made the right decision.

Back to their argument, though. Asher's right. Despite that initial glow of the surrogate news, Lilly hasn't been herself. I knew about the drinking, the nights out, and the excessive spending, but this fooling around business is new to me.

"I didn't mean it," she says to me now. "The part about not wanting to be a mom. I want the baby, Kinsley."

I don't respond.

"I'm not proud of who I've become. My behavior's deplorable."

I sip water.

She wipes the donut grease from her hands and takes the seat beside me. She starts to touch my belly but I grab her wrist and squeeze.

She flinches.

The first time I hurt Lilly had been an impulse—my reaction to her deleting my work. For once I felt like I had the upper hand. Like my whole life hadn't been forfeited for my sister.

Since then, there have been many other times…

"Get your shit together." I squeeze tighter.

Lilly cringes. "I will. I promise."

————

Three weeks later via cesarean section, I give birth to a healthy baby girl. They name her Tessa, after our mother.

CHAPTER 21

 *arch, Present Day*

As expected, the movie adaptation of *Sister Sister* swept the Oscars.

After, Lilly and the director were stopped for interviews.

A reporter was saying, "Lilly, you have reinvented the art of storytelling. You are a true master of your craft. Your writing surpasses all others. What can we expect next from Lilly Day?"

With a humble smile, Lilly responded with the words Kinsley told her to say while Kinsley stood in the shadows watching.

Beside her, someone quietly commented, "I would give my big toe to have her gifted mind."

———

They were now at one of the many after-parties where Lilly was expected to make an appearance. This one was being hosted at a vast Beverly Hills estate elaborately decorated with glittering vases full of flowers and crystal halo chandleries. Servers circulated with gleaming gold trays handing out endless glasses of champagne.

Lilly stood over in the corner surrounded by the producer, director, actors, and various others. Everyone talked loudly, reveling in the awards.

Not Lilly, though. She stood quietly, completely checked out, having already slammed way too many champagnes.

Kinsley spotted Julian in a separate corner talking to no one as he too worked on total inebriation.

Short of forcing them to leave, there wasn't much Kinsley could do. Not in front of all these people.

Lilly finished a glass. A server instantly appeared giving her another. She needed to eat something.

Kinsley flagged down a waiter with a tray of appetizers. "Please make sure Ms. Day eats something."

With a nod, the waiter crossed the room. He offered Lilly food. She shook her head. He said something to her. She looked across the room at Kinsley, reluctantly taking an appetizer and shoving it into her mouth.

In her peripheral, Kinsley saw Julian stumbling through the crowd, heading toward her. He staggered into her personal space. His words came slurred. "You and me?" He swayed. "We're in this together."

"Julian, you're drunk."

He chuckled. "I know that."

A clinking glass filtered through the air. Gradually, the crowd grew silent. "Speech. Speech. Speech." They begin to chant.

The director went up the grand staircase, taking Lilly with him. They stopped halfway. Her hand came out, latching onto the curved banister. "I'm a little drunk."

The crowd laughed.

"Speech. Speech. Speech."

The director cleared his throat. He spoke.

Holding a flute of champagne, she blearily stared down into it, probably not even listening to the director's words. After giving a brief speech where he thanked everyone involved, he looked at her. "Now let's hear from the woman who penned such a moving book that inspired my vision."

Lilly licked her lips. But she didn't speak. She just kept staring at the half empty flute.

Julian wobbled. "Yes, let's hear what the *great* Lilly Day has to say."

His voice came too loud. Several people shot him an odd look.

Kinsley turned fully to face him. "Shut. Up."

His glassy eyes widened. He stared at her. A weird second ticked by. His mouth opened. Kinsley saw the moment he realized that *she* held control. She wasn't the poor, taken-advantage-of-sister that he thought.

A throat cleared.

Kinsley swiveled away from Julian, looking back at Lilly who now stared at her over the tops of everyone's heads. Kinsley nodded, encouraging her sister to speak.

"Um, sorry." Nervously, Lilly laughed. "I'm usually pretty good at giving speeches. But I find myself without words. I'm overcome with emotion."

Unfortunately, she finished the rest of her drink. Her eyes swept the crowd. "First, thank you for this lovely party. I am incredibly grateful. All of this though is because of Kinsley, my sister."

The rustling of people turning to look at Kinsley filled the room. She gave a modest nod, immediately going back to her sister. Kinsley's steely gaze fastened on Lilly.

Lilly continued, "The thing is, she's in my brain all the time. I don't have a thought without her putting it there. She's the yin to my yang. She saves me from myself. She makes it possible for all of this to happen. She helps to quiet my noisy mind. Because of her, the words appear on the screen. Her sanity and focus keep me on track. So, I'd like to make a toast to my sister."

People exchanged a confused look.

Lilly lifted an empty glass. "To Kinsley, my maker."

CHAPTER 22

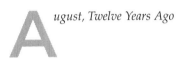

August, Twelve Years Ago

Pregnant with Lilly and Asher's second baby, I sit in the home office, my fingers racing over the keys, putting the final touches on book number five. I wish I could get back to the days when I luxuriously handwrote my novels. I do feel more creative that way.

Lilly stands to the side of me, holding a fan directly on my face. This pregnancy has caused nonstop hot flashes.

With a sigh, she shifts from one foot to the next.

Furiously, I type.

With another sigh, she shifts back.

I stay focused.

"Are you thirsty?" she asks.

"No." I keep going.

"Hungry?"

"No."

The keys click. The words fly.

Another sigh. She shifts back.

I stop typing. Moving only my hand I reach over and pinch her upper thigh, twisting the skin. "If it's that much problem for you to stand there and hold a fan on your *pregnant* sister while she writes *your* novel, then find something to prop it up with."

"I'm sorry," she quickly says. "Please."

The office door flies open. I release her thigh. Two-year-old Tessa runs in. "Mommy, Mommy, Mommy."

Lilly plants a big grin on her face as she puts the fan down. She picks up Tessa. "Mommy's working. Where's Daddy?"

I refocus. I read the last few lines, then begin typing again.

"I'm here." Asher comes in. He takes Tessa from Lilly's arms. He pauses. "I thought you said you were writing."

"I am. Kinsley's editing a few of my things."

"Oh…" Asher backs out, leaving us alone. "I'll leave you to it then."

Lilly's grin falls away. She rubs her thigh. "When will we ever be even?"

"Considering you've never once done a thing for me? Never. Now, fan," I snap.

Quickly she picks it up and points it at my face.

I continue typing.

CHAPTER 23

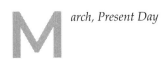

March, Present Day

After the speech, someone escorted Lilly down the steps. Multiple people moved toward her but she ignored them all as she headed toward the way out.

Kinsley followed

A server carrying an enormous tray heavy with appetizers came through an archway as Lilly crossed in front. They collided. The tray clattered to the marble floor. Food flew, a good majority of it landing on Lilly. She tripped and fell.

The area quieted.

People swept in, helping her stand and also trying to clean her dress. A man offered her a cloth napkin. She jerked away, stumbling toward the exit.

Kinsley picked up pace.

Outside, Lilly flagged down their limo. She climbed inside. Kinsley ducked in behind her.

Lilly growled. "Leave me alone."

"What are you doing?"

"Leaving."

"You can't just leave. This whole party is for you."

"Watch me."

"You're being a child."

She folded her arms. The driver got behind the wheel and pulled away.

"You left your purse. Not to mention your Oscar for co-producer."

"Don't you mean *your* Oscar?"

Kinsley jabbed her finger on the button that controlled the privacy screen. It glided upward. Lilly picked a shrimp stuck to her dress and flung it to the floor.

"Fine. I'll text Julian to get your things. We'll go back to the hotel. I'll make you a pot of coffee. We'll get you sobered up. We'll get you a new dress. Hell, I'll give you *my* dress."

Lilly glared at Kinsley. "I don't think you heard me. I'm done. I'm going home. I want you gone. Effective immediately, you no longer live with us. I'm not doing any more books. Or rather you're not. I'll tell Julian tomorrow. He can find a new author to manage. I'm done. I mean it. We're going to go to a lawyer and negotiate a buyout for you. You and me, we're over."

———

They arrived at the hotel. Lilly charged through the lobby and straight into the elevator. Kinsley followed quickly on her heels. She punched the button for the roof before Lilly pressed the button for their floor.

"What are you doing?" Lilly snapped.

"You can't go back into our suite, not with Tessa and Enid there. You need to get yourself under control."

Lilly's mouth snapped closed. She gave a jerky nod.

Neither spoke as the elevator ascended. It opened to the

rooftop pool. They stepped out onto a veranda, empty and hushed for the night. Voluminous white curtains were drawn and tied, giving the terrace an Arabian feel. A mild breeze rippled across the pool's surface.

Lilly paced away.

Silently, Kinsley watched her.

Lilly said, "The name Lilly Day has grown into a beast."

"That's what you wanted, remember?"

"Yes, but not this way."

"We're partners," Kinsley said. "You're the face. I'm the talent. There's nothing wrong with that."

"All we've done is lie. Do you think I'm proud of that? I'm not. You've manipulated and controlled me, and I've let you."

"*I've* manipulated and controlled you? I believe you're the one who started that."

"And bravo to you for outmaneuvering me."

"It's not like that."

"Yes, it is," Lilly said. "And you know it is."

Kinsley took a breath. "Lilly, we're sisters. We love each other for better or worse. It's always been you and me. It always will be you and me. It takes both of us to make this work. Sacrificing for each other is what we do. Comforting each other is what we do. Hell, I carried both of your babies. We have one another's backs, always. Our relationship may be twisted, but somehow it works."

Lilly scoffed. "For who?" She stopped pacing the pool. "I know I took advantage of you. Your name should have been on those books. I should have never allowed it otherwise. But haven't I made up for that? Are you going to continue to punish me until the day I die?"

Lilly held both arms out. "Or do you want to break one of my wrists again?"

She pulled her hair up, showing the back of her neck. "Or maybe you want to burn me again with a curling iron."

She lifted her blue dress, exposing her thighs. "Or how about a good. Hard. Pinch. Will that make you feel better?"

Yes. "You've always been selfish," Kinsley said. "I allowed it. Hell, I even nurtured it. I helped to create the self-absorbed woman you've become."

"And I helped create the sociopathic woman you've become."

"Because of my 'sociopathic behavior' and our warped relationship I've fashioned masterpieces that critics will rave after we're both in the grave."

"Masterpieces?" Lilly snorted. "Look at your swollen ego."

"I'm only repeating what others say."

"Whatever. I can do just as well, given a true chance."

"Really?" Kinsley asked, making sure Lilly heard the snark in that one word. "You wanted this. The money. The first-class travel. The five-star treatment. The fame. You love being waited on. You love being loved. I never once cared."

"Leave me alone. I don't want to 'talk this out' or whatever it is we're doing."

"No."

"You know what your problem is? You hate that out in public you're in my shadow. You've always been there. You resent the humiliation of being my 'assistant.' Even if your name headlined the books you'd be a fumbling idiot in interviews. Don't get me started on signings. You'd be this moronic stoic author that no one ever wanted to see again. My personality has rocketed us. Has sustained us."

"You are a vain talentless bitch."

Lilly's head reeled as if Kinsley slapped her. Call Lilly a narcissistic twat and she laughed. But call her talentless and it touched a nerve.

Quiet seconds beat by. Kinsley paced around the pool, her gaze steady. She waited for her words to crush. To beat Lilly into submission. To fill her full of so much doubt that no words came. Instead, anger whirled in her eyes.

Kinsley stopped in front of her. Lilly turned fully to face her.

She said, "I want you to tell me what happened with Asher."

CHAPTER 24

*J*une, Five Years Ago

My fingers cruise over the keys as I excitedly draft book number nine, *Sister Sister*. This novel had initially been Lilly's idea. At the time though I told her to wait. It needed more history before it saw the page.

Now is the time.

Sure it'll be a best seller and optioned for film, just like most of the others; but this one will snag the Pulitzer. Watch.

On the large monitor in front of me, the words appear. They spill from me fast. This book doesn't come out until early next year, but pre-orders are already "through the roof" as Julian said.

My stomach growls, reminding me it's time for lunch.

Just a few more lines…

I click save. I breathe out. I can't remember the last time I felt such energy for creating a story.

Stretching my arms over my head, I roll my neck. I stand and stretch. I take a few luxurious seconds to stare out the expansive windows at the ocean, sparkling prettily in the late morning sun. I love this house. I'm glad Lilly and Asher decided to build it. Lilly calls it their "forever" home. I still live in the condo I've lived in for years. Can I afford a different place? Sure, but why? The condo suits me just fine. Besides, I spend nearly all day every day here at their place.

I turn, ready to raid the kitchen, and I freeze.

Asher stands there, staring at the large screen monitor.

I step in front of it, blocking his view. "I thought you were at the hospital."

His rigid gaze latches onto me. "I knew it."

"Knew what?"

"That you write Lilly's books."

I don't deny it. So what if Asher knows?

"All those times you two used to lock the door so you could 'work.' How she gives you half of her advance, jokingly telling me you're the most overpaid assistant. Why half the time she seems clueless about the books she wrote. I knew it."

"I thought you were at the hospital," I repeat.

"The cops are there questioning if I'm the one who broke her wrist." He takes an intimidating step toward me. "It's you, isn't it? The stitches last year where she 'accidentally' stabbed her hand with a pairing knife. The constant bruising on her thighs that she claims is from her strength training class. The multiple burns on the back of her neck where she just can't seem to work a curling iron correctly."

"What can I say, your wife's a klutz."

"I want you gone. Get out of my house."

"You better be nice to me. If the cops ask, I'll put lots of suspicious doubt in their minds."

"Get out!"

"No."

He lunges across the office and grabs my upper arm. It's so quick and unexpected I don't have time to think before he pushes me out into the hall. He shoves me toward the stairwell.

I swing around, landing a hard slap across his cheek. He shoves me again. I kick back. My heel connects with his shin. He grunts. I go for his throat ready to choke when he gets another shove in. My knees hit the tile flooring. I grimace. He yanks me to my feet and shoves me again. I'm now at the top of the stairwell. I whirl around, not sure where I'm going to aim. But I punch. My fist meets the air as he ducks. He's on the other side of me now, closer to the stairs. He rotates to face me as I push his shoulders with both of my hands. His eyes widen. His body momentarily catches air. Then he falls.

Head over feet.

Side over side.

Body bouncing.

Twenty tiled steps in all to land hard on the polished floor. His skull cracks so loudly against the solid surface that it fills the foyer with an echoing crunch.

Breathing hard, I stare down.

Asher is dead.

CHAPTER 25

arch, Present Day

Lilly didn't remember grabbing her sister.

She didn't remember the vice grip her fingers took.

The struggle.

Or pushing Kinsley, just like she pushed Asher.

All she remembered was the scream as she went over the parapet...

It echoed still in her skull. It ricocheted around in her brain. It hammered through her body.

Lilly stood at the roof's edge, numbly looking down eight stories to where her sister landed on the concrete, one leg bent at an odd angle. Blood pooled under her sister's head.

Sirens blared. Hotel staff rushed around. No one noticed Lilly on the roof. Slowly, she backed away from the edge. She sat cross-legged on the pool deck. She stared out at the night's clear sky.

Her heart hurt. Her breaths came quickly. She pressed

both hands, one on top of the other, into her chest. Her body stilled.

Then helpless terror vibrated through her. What had she done?

She vaguely registered the door to the roof opening.

"Ms. Day? Ms. Day? Are you alright?" Someone came down beside her. A soothing hand stroked across her upper back.

Lilly closed her eyes. The terror faded. Unspeakable sorrow flooded her soul.

She registered the sound of more feet coming onto the roof.

"Is she okay?"

"What happened?"

"Ms. Day?"

"Can you hear me?"

"Are you hurt?"

Lilly slumped forward. Her arms wound around her middle. Her eyes squeezed tighter still. Her body began to rock.

She cried.

EPILOGUE

September, Present Day

Six months transpired since Lilly pushed Kinsley off that roof.

Lilly told the police that Kinsley was leaning over the parapet and fell. Just like she'd once told the police that Asher tripped at the top of the staircase.

They transported Kinsley's body back to Florida. After a beautiful ceremony, they laid her to rest next to their parents.

Julian attended that ceremony. After, he and Lilly decided to part ways. They issued a press release that Lilly Day had written her last book. They also decided to keep the real author's identity a secret between the two of them.

Though Lilly spent years being abused by Kinsley, she still missed her sister. Their relationship, though once loving and sisterly, grew into a dysfunctional monster. Lilly fully recognized her part in it.

Now Lilly spent her days focused on her daughters, making up for years of absent motherhood. She worked hard at rebuilding her relationship with Tessa and Enid.

Sometimes when Lilly was all alone, she'd lay on the beach and hold the beaded *Forever Sisters* necklace. Lilly would stare up at the night sky and recall a night long ago when they first lost their parents.

The sisters lay side by side on a blanket in the front yard of their foster home. They held hands as they stared up at the dark sky.

"Why are we doing this?" Kinsley asked.

"Shh, just wait."

They did, for what seemed forever. Then, it happened. Not one shooting star, but two.

Lilly pointed. "There they are. Mom and Dad. That means they're angels now."

Yes, Lilly would lay on the beach and watch for Kinsley's shooting star.

But one never came.

BOOKS BY S. E. GREEN

The Family

Be careful what you wish for…

The Lady Next Door

How well do you know your neighbor?

Killers Among

Lane swore never to be like her late mother. But now she too is a serial killer.

Monster

When the police need to crawl inside the mind of a monster, they call Caroline.

The Third Son

All he wants is a loving family to belong to, to manipulate, to control…

Vanquished

A secret island. A sadistic society. And the woman who defies all odds to bring it down.

Mother May I

Meet Nora: Flawless. Enigmatic. Conniving. Ruthless.

ABOUT THE AUTHOR

S. E. Green is the award-winning, best-selling author of young adult and adult fiction. She grew up in Tennessee where she dreaded all things reading and writing. She didn't read her first book for enjoyment until she was twenty-five. After that, she was hooked! When she's not writing, she loves traveling and hanging out with a rogue armadillo that frequents her coastal Florida home.

Manufactured by Amazon.ca
Bolton, ON

40242905R00067